The Three Kings of Ybor

Volume 4: August the 18th

Written By Rock Kitaro

www.StageInTheSky.com

Copyright 2015

**Photos provided by Jen Poblete
and Brandy Scaglione of Exposition Photography**

Table of Contents

Chapter 14 – Strike One: Playing the House   6

Chapter 15 – Strike Two: Breaking the Bank   39

Chapter 16 – Strike Three: The Port of St. Petersburg 83

Recap of "The Three Kings of Ybor – Volume 4: A Reunion of Beasts"

On the rooftops high above a sea of flesh and revelry, the intrepid Eliza Christie finally crosses blades with her father's murderer, Braden Pierce. Joining the fray to aide Eliza is yet another master swordsman, the private investigator Gavin Hassell. With all three combatants possessing enhanced strength and senses as Furyx Users, they put on a spectacular swordfight in which thousands of club hoppers and half-drunken pedestrians bear witness.

These witnesses immediately take to social media and underground forums, launching the "Three Kings of Ybor" legend and making the unknown swordsmen an overnight viral phenomenon with fans growing by the thousands every day. Eliza reveals to fellow college freshmen Robby McCloud that she is one of the Three Kings and openly admits that she plans on destroying the Pierce Syndicate no matter the cost.

After Robby enlightens her with the flaws of those who have tried before her, Eliza devises a plan to round up local ex-military and disheartened law enforcement officers. She has Robby send an encrypted e-mail with a powerful message, one that chokes at the conscience and rekindles their passion to stand up for what's right in the face of death. Out of the hundreds who received the message, only fifty show up. Fifty men who have lost loved ones to the fangs of the Pierce Syndicate.

Eliza shows them what she can do. She proves that she is more than capable. She takes command of her underground militia, christening them with the title of the very book that inspired her to pick herself up when she was spiraling down a pit of despair. The adventures of August the 18th are about to begin.

Warning: The following contains graphic violence and plausible profanity.

Chapter 14 – Strike One: Playing the House

The first semester of college started on the first week of September. Temperatures were already starting to drop to below forty. Needless to say, the first few weeks of September were hectic for Eliza and Robby. Tasked with keeping up the appearances of good hard working students, the duo also had to accelerate the progress of beginning their official activities as the leaders of August the 18th. Following the suggestions of Robby and former intelligence officer Brian Wells, the first priority on a long list of tasks to do was fortifying the Oldsmar warehouse as their designated headquarters.

On a frigid cold afternoon when Robby finished up his first day of class, he found himself sitting on an old wooden bench in front of the warehouse. The screen of the open laptop in his lap showed an elevated camera view, but it was obstructed with heavy static interference. The surveillance feed showed the eastern view of Langston Road going away from their Oldsmar warehouse. With a skeptical grimace, Robby looked up at an abandoned building across the street from his position.

Sinus was on top of this rooftop with two other 18th volunteers who had the afternoon off. While dressed warmly in civilian attire they made sure to wear electrical gloves for safety. Using their combined knowledge of electrical circuits and signal processing, they worked with confidence repairing the outdated CCTV camera. Mainly, all they needed to do was replace the dirty lens and faulty wiring. Each of them had an earpiece given to them by Robby. It was Robby providing proper instruction and confirming or disapproving their guesses on the spot like a ten-year supervisor. Despite being told that they were wrong more than once, the three grown men took Robby's advice with a grain of salt.

"I appreciate this, you guys." Robby said through the earpiece, probably predicting Sinus's frustration.

No one responded.

"Yeah, besides setting up cameras and security inside our own fortress, I thought it would probably be a good idea to tap into our neighbor's cameras. I have a fear of snipers, ya know? Or even being trapped for that matter." Robby said with a chuckle.

Sinus rolled his eyes. "It's okay Robby. I'm glad to help. Just tell me what to do." He said calmly in a mild Korean dialect, carefully trying his best to pronounce each word, one word at a time.

"Alright hold it! Whatever you just did, leave it alone. We're good. Ha! It's awesome." Robby exclaimed.

"Good goddamn it!" The man next to Sinus barked out loud.

Sinus looked further down the barren Langston Road to an abandoned cement factory. The tall ghostly Priest Edwin was on top of one of the silos, setting up another surveillance camera. He too had to cut out exposed damaged wires, but he didn't seem as frustrated as Sinus's crew and he enjoyed the solitude.

"How are we, Robby?" Priest asked in his usually raspy voice that sent chills down Robby's spine.

"Yeah man, we're good... Jesus..." Robby confirmed.
...

In downtown Tampa, former SWAT captain James Slater was on the graveyard shift manning the armory checkout counter in the police department garage. The cops on the night shift clocked in at eight and headed out to patrol the streets so that by ten, there was hardly any activity at the checkout counter. It was then that Slater allowed Brian Wells and several off duty officers, all soldiers of August the 18th, to stroll in and head for the back ammunitions archive room.

The archive room was where broken, outdated or defective weapons and equipment came to collect dust and provide nostalgia. The 18th soldiers entered the archive room dressed in dark clothing, but not wearing masks. If any official just so happens to walk by, Slater would give them a nod signaling that nothing was out of the ordinary.

It was Robby who persuaded an overly apprehensive Slater to allow August the 18th to basically steal the equipment. He told him, "Since most of you guys are cops or ex-cops, it'd be cool if you used your weight to get weapons, body armor, and any security clearance codes you can get your hands on. I'll hack the cameras, but we still need people who look like cops to get in there just in case."

And while outspoken Slater still wore his concerns on his sleeve, it was Eliza who'd put him in place with guilt-wreaking statements like, "You're willing to put your life on the line, but not your job?"

Eliza and Robby were attending a class that same night. With over 120 students studying in groups for Interpersonal Communication, it was easy for them to remain under the radar as they sat in the back of the classroom. Each student had their own laptop. On Robby's laptop, he could see the surveillance footage of a hacked camera inside the TMPD garage. He watched as Slater, Brian and four other 18th men loaded large duffle bags with all kinds of gadgets, ranging from electrical spears, decommissioned assault rifles, grenades, and grappling guns.

The sight of it all was so stimulating to Robby. It was as if he was finally allowed to ride the big rides at an amusement park. More and more he got into the spirit of things, believing in what the group could potentially do. Full of boisterous confidence and authority was Slater's usual demeanor so it was comical for Robby to see him unusually nervous. The authoritative thirty-something year old was constantly looking around like a paranoid cat, jumping at any unidentified sound. Smirking with laughter, Robby couldn't resist but to pull an earpiece out of his book bag and put it on.

"Come on Slater, don't be like that. Chillax man!" Robby snickered.

Slater heard him through his own earpiece and looked around for a camera. He found it directly above Brian in the corner of the room. Pissed off and frustrated, Slater raised his middle finger up to the camera. Robby burst out into a hysterical cackling laughter before leaning over to get Eliza's attention.

"Look man! He's so uptight. How can I not stop myself from cracking on him?" He said.

Eliza was intensely focused on her own laptop. To appease Robby, she quickly glanced over and threw an entertained smile to shut him up. On her screen she was reading a news report about how a Florida Senator was recently acquitted of gambling charges. The state Senator was accused of illegally gambling on underage girl fights that resulted in the death of six elementary students. Those fights took place at the popular Majestic Vault Casino in the recreation district of Hyde Park. The fights were managed and promoted by the casino's very own executive vice president. A woman named Sofia Monteiro.

Eliza read in anger as she found out that the casino was closed down for only a week for investigations before it was reopened again. Sofia Monteiro spent only two days in jail before being released on bail. In a press conference, the unremorseful Monteiro declared that she had no intention of stepping down from her corporate post and worse… she blamed the parents for the deaths of those six girls due to negligence. So for the rest of the night, Eliza festered with her fingertips gently caressing the handle of her ninja sword, Ivy.

By the second Saturday of that September, the 18th members were beginning to feel like a real team. They were learning more about each other and cliques of friendships were beginning to sprout. Brian, in particular had a huge influence on Eliza's leadership. As if she was his pupil, he began to train her to think and investigate like an Imperial Intelligence officer. He challenged her perception by encouraging her to spot deception and look beyond the obvious evidence.

In one section of their Oldsmar warehouse, six burly men with tattoos and proud beards wore protective facemasks as they carefully spray-painted the confiscated body armor and weapons on the floor. As per Eliza's orders, she wanted everyone and everything to display the dark color of Army green. It was to be their calling card. A symbol of unity and solidarity.

On another side of the warehouse, a cage was set up to create an MMA octagon ring. Body bags and punching dummies were stationed to create a practice area. A group of about twenty men had gathered around Priest Edwin for a demonstration. Even though Priest Edwin's primary expertise was with an electric-powered scoped sniper rifle, he showed surprising skill in demonstrating how to fight with a spear. Everyone watched as he twirled the long slender spear with such grace, dishing out swift overhead and vertical strikes while spinning as if he was performing a ballet.

Sinus was amongst them. He sat silently watching from a corner, impressed, but not blown away. After the demonstration, several of the onlookers applauded the Priest. But Sinus approached with a smile, gesturing for Priest to give him some room. Everyone respected the chivalry and cheered for the mysterious Sinus to show them something new. Sinus took off his hooded jean jacket and grabbed hold of the Korean broadsword that was strapped to his back. With a powerful swing that whistled through the air, he began his demonstration showing off an impressive array of Chinese stances and acrobatic flips with the blade. Everyone rooted, greatly appreciating the competitive display.

Soon after, on a Sunday morning, Eliza, Brian and Robby visited a used car dealership with their heart's set on purchasing several thick panel unmarked vans. As they stood in the lobby, your typical compensated by commission sales representative approached.

"Hello and welcome to Pinellas Family Owned Vehicles. My name is Georgiano! Is there anything I can help you with today?" The sales rep asked, mainly talking to Brian who he assumed to be the father.

"Thanks but we're here to just look around and see what you guys have to offer. Are you running any specials as far as interest rates and financing?" Brian asked him.

While Brian engaged the eager Georgiano in conversation, Eliza was looking outside the lobby window toward some older light green hummers parked in the lot. The instant she set her eyes on the large tank-like vehicles, her heart was set.

"Oh I see, I see. Well if I may make a suggestion..." The sales rep began.

Robby noticed the sales rep clasping his fingers together, leaning forward with a flirting vibe towards Brian. He couldn't help but to raise his hands to cover his grin as he looked away.

"We do have a very good special that you can take advantage of for your son and daughter. It's an extension of our Labor Day Special." Georgiano told them.

"How many of those do you have?" Eliza asked, referring to the hummers.

The sales rep walked over to view Eliza's line of vision. "Hummers? Um…I'm not sure exactly. But I do know we have three, all in that color. But we can re-paint them to any color you'd like."

Taking note of Eliza's obvious want for the vehicles, Brian quickly asked, "So how much is the interest rate on…"

"We'll take em. All of them." Eliza said. Brian gave her a stern look. Eliza returned with a smile suggesting that everything will be all right.

"Good. Good. I'll go get the paperwork ready." Georgiano said before hurrying off.

"Yeah, you go do that. I wonder if he'll skip on his way back." Robby joked.

Brian shook his head at Eliza. "Damn it, Eliza. You didn't even know how much they cost."

"Doesn't matter. I want them." Eliza said as she patted him on the back.

"Yep. That's our commander. No finesse. No subtleties. No poker face at all. Just straight-forward and blunt. Love it." Brian said under his breath, inducing a smirk from Eliza.

…

On October 1st, 2206, the members of August the 18th had gathered for the briefing of their first official mission. Preparations were complete. Their warehouse now looked like a fully furnished military compound. There was a lounge area complete with a couch set, beverage cabinets and a big screen monitor usually set to the local news station. They had a communications area with monitors that could be set to any CCTV camera in the city with the click of a remote. There were four computers stations set up with illegal access to satellite communications systems, international domain names and government databases.

The three large hummers were parked inside the warehouse and coated with a new layer of dark-green metallic paint. Four other members volunteered their vehicles for the ready if ever it were necessary. And every vehicle was registered under one of the dozens of aliases Brian used in the service. The vehicles were fitted with an electronic jamming device that virtually made their image invisible to satellites and police radar scanners. Robby was meticulous. He spent days testing the vehicles to make sure the jamming devices worked and even then, he was still nervous about using them. If a patrol car happened to drive by with their radars not picking up the Hummer's signal, that's just cause for a traffic stop. Very inconvenient.

By this point, Eliza had already filled in the group on the effects of the Furyx Gene and displayed enough of her abilities to show a fraction of her potential. She also made Brian, Slater, Priest Edwin and Sinus captains and divided the group into four units over which the captains would lead.

Following Brian's suggestion, Eliza was wearing a fire resistant version of the dark-green hooded overcoat that she seemed obsessed with wearing almost every single day. In addition to her Ivy sword and the assortment of small ninja weaponry, Eliza was given a set of grenades that Priest Edwin fashioned by fusing her ninja stars with gunpowder. All she would have to do is press a button with the strength that only someone of her ability could muster. She'd then have to get rid of it within seven seconds.

During the briefing, Eliza was standing on a platform, fully dressed in her field uniform. Her ventilated facemask was hanging from her neck as she addressed the entire group of 18th soldiers, all who stood in front of her in military fashion. Every masked 18th soldier was dressed in their own dark-green choice of all-terrain fatigues, their choice of weapons, their choice of spray-painted body armor and they were all wearing a communications earpiece. Robby was the only one standing off to the side of her, dressed in his casual street clothes and signature trucker hat.

Eliza began her war speech in a deep bass-heavy voice. "Every casino in the city are all in some way associated with foul play. There's not a single lawful one amongst them. They steal from the public and get rid of anyone who brings forth evidence of their corruption. Well…Let's see them try and get rid of us tonight!" Eliza shouted. The men of the 18th pumped their fists with a boisterous war cry.

"Tonight, delivering a message is our goal. They will know the name August the 18th and from this day forward…They will learn to fear us. Just as normal hardworking citizens who work to provide food and shelter for their families fear walking down the wrong road to keep from becoming a statistic or picture on the six o'clock news. Just as legitimate business owners and employees fear becoming too successful to keep from drawing the wrong sort of attention. Children, used as smugglers. Women, sold into becoming sex slaves. Men, forced to become drug mules. Police officers who are all well aware of who and where the rapists and serial killers are, but are too afraid to take a stand and put them behind bars because it would only paint a target on their backs."

"Gentlemen, tonight…We show the syndicate and the entire world that every man and woman has a breaking point. No longer will we prostrate ourselves and become the bricks that pave the streets they walk on. We are the wall that obstructs their paths of domination. We are the phoenixes that have risen amongst the ashes of their victims. We didn't ask for this. We're not vigilantes. We are not law enforcement. We are simply individuals who are no longer sitting back and accepting things are just the way they are."

Eliza looked into the eyes of her men. Everyone shared the same conviction, the same belief. She wasn't sure if the word's she chose would be remembered for some speech or for the history books, but it was the only truth she was able to convey. After letting half a minute go by, Eliza stepped down off the platform and gestured for Brian Wells to take over. Captain Wells lowered his facemask, stepped forward and turned around to address the group. Meanwhile Eliza and Robby separated and headed for the communications area.

"All right, gentlemen. No civilian casualties will be tolerated unless they show aggression. We've been over the schematics of the Majestic Vault Casino. You know your assignments. Let's wheel up." He told them.

Eliza watched as the group dispersed. Her heart was pounding. It was just in her nature to mentally prepare herself for everything that could possibly go wrong. With only a small amount of chatter, the men were filing into either one of the three hummers or their own green painted armored vehicles. Robby stationed himself in front of a desktop computer station and grabbed his pair of computerized goggles hung from his backpack. These goggles allowed him to browse any network by using the electric sensors in his black gloves. He looked up to Eliza and could see a small trace of uncertainty in her eyes as she pulled her hair back into a topknot.

"Hey." Robby whispered to get her attention. "You'll do fine, Eliza. Remember your convictions. Remember your father. You're the leader of August the 18th. Go out there and lead."

Eliza nodded. "You'll stay online?"

"Yep. I'll be your eyes and ears, disabling camera feeds and warning you of incoming opposition wherever they may spawn." Robby assured her with a confident grin.

Eliza's smile faded on and off. "Good."

After covering her head with the hood of her coat, she turned and strutted towards the hummers. Again Robby found himself with his arms crossed, watching her proudly. It was a magnificent scene. The young female commander draped in a coat that looked like a cloak, walking toward shining headlights of the hummers. The harmonious sounds of the engines, the solid knocks as Eliza's boots strutted across the rubber flooring. It was all so cool. With an excited smile, Robby put on his goggles and a thick headset that allowed him to hear and speak with the 18th soldiers.

Eliza entered the front passenger seat of the hummer with Slater as the driver. Brian and two other 18th men were in the back seat while two more men were sitting in the truck bed. One by one the vehicles began to pull out of the warehouse's garage doors.

"Alright ladies and gentlemen, or rather gentlemen and one sexy lady with legs as high the sky down to the floor. This is your friendly neighborhood techie, providing a smooth ride, an eye in the sky, and some smooth background music to put your minds at ease." Robby said through their earpieces in a cartoonish voice.

"Keep the lines clear, asshole. Stop all the goddamn chatter." Slater barked as he was backing up the hummer.

"And that, my friends, is my feisty girlfriend, Captain James Slater. I am working on his hostility issues, but you can't blame him if it's that time of the month. HOWEVER! PMS is no excuse when you're out in the field. So I don't want no back talk else I'll have to come out there and take off my belt!" Robby continued in his cartoonish voice.

The humor was sorely needed to break the icy tension. Both Eliza and Brian couldn't help but smirk as the other men chuckled hopelessly. Slater simply shook his head and mumbled threats under his breath. The vehicles convoy began down the road with the clock set at just a little half past nine.

With the hummers gone, Robby knew that it was about a thirty-minute ETA. Pushing his luck, he decided to put on some dark energetic techno to blast through the members earpieces. Fortunately, the music was well received. As the three hummers and two pickup trucks cruised the relatively light traffic of Hillsborough Avenue heading east, most of the 18th men bobbed their heads as they checked their stun guns, their Tec-9s, their swords and daggers and spears…all clearing their minds to get their heads in the game.

Through his computerized goggles, Robby was able to keep his eyes on eight different monitors, moving one to the side and pulling up another with the motion of his gloves. His eyes were peeled on the bird's eye satellite view of the convoy. They stayed within the speed limit so as to not draw any attention. Robby would've warned them of any impending patrol cars.

As expected on a Friday night, the closer they drove into the city towards the grand Majestic Vault Casino, the crazier the traffic became. The flashing lights, honking horns and musical streets got the men ready. Only Brian and Slater carried assault rifles. They couldn't afford metal shells, but ballistic rubber pellets would work for the job. As they approached the casino, the men caught sight of the spectacular geysers that spewed fires straight up into the sky. Everyone knew these were the famous geysers that rimmed along the edges of the front driveway entrance of the casino.

"All right everyone. This is it!" Slater shouted.

At speeds of over 50mph, Slater sped the convoy boldly towards the front driveway, honking his horn and flashing his high beams to herd bystanders out of the way. Several security guards standing near the entrance caught sight of them and immediately held up their radio handsets requesting for backup. Nobody responded. Robby was jamming the frequency of their communication sets.

The hummers and pickup trucks came to a screeching halt directly in the middle of the half-moon driveway entrance. Eliza was the first one out. With the swift speed of a jaguar, she sprinted forward until she was within twenty feet of the nearest security guards. Then with a whipping wave of her right arm, she released a flurry of ninja stars that lodged into the necks of three security guards in uniforms. A party of five scantily-clad cougars screamed in horror as the men dropped to their knees with blood gushing from their necks.

"Eliza! Jesus! Those security guards could be just doing their jobs. What happened to no casualties?" Robby barked.

Eliza briefly glanced at the wounded men and rolled her eyes. "Flesh wounds, Robby."

Twenty-eight August the 18th soldiers quickly rushed out of the vehicles with four remaining to stand guard. In double file formation, Eliza led Brian and Slater, then Sinus and Priest Edwin, followed by the rest of them through the sliding glass doors that was the entrance, completely ignoring the security guards who was choking for help.

The obnoxious ringing and jingles of hundreds of slot machines going off at once made it hard for them to hear their own earpieces. The dazzling gold and green shamrock themed casino floor was packed with every sort of gambler, manic depressant and frivolous spender imaginable. Everyone in their middle-ages was dressed as if their prime era fashion sense never went out of style. Everyone in their 20s was dressed promiscuously as if they openly welcomed sex, first come first serve.

Brian and Slater raised their assault rifles and sprayed loud rubber bullets toward the ceiling. Scared out of their minds, everyone on the packed floor room ducked down and turned to the gunmen. Keeping in stride, the group continued to follow Eliza's strut down the main aisle of the floor as if they were conducting a legitimate imperial raid.

"Alright everyone, sit down and shut up and we won't have a problem. We're not here for you. So don't make your night any worse than it already is." Brian shouted calmly.

"Hey! Everyone shut the fuck up! Hey! You! Sit your ass down! Move woman! Get those titties covered up before I slap em. Bouncing around like this is goddamn a water-balloon fight. The hell you think this is?" Slater shouted more aggressively almost at the same time as Brian.

In the casino's security room there were six uniformed humanoid androids monitoring the twenty-six monitor screens with four human supervisors. Android 7-C instantly alerted the head supervisor, Marvick. Marvick then instantly set off the alarm to lock the place down and notify the authorities. And just as he was ordering a facial recognition scan to see if the program could bypass the 18th's facemasks, one by one, the computer screens turned to static. As shock and confusion washed over the employees, the static was replaced with Robby's taunting screensaver of an anime style cartoon character of a boy wearing a red trucker hat and a get-under-your-skin grin.

By now, Eliza was leading the group toward a fork in the walkway. The left path led to the blackjack and craps tables, the right pathway headed towards the theater and restaurants. They needed to pass through the theater and restaurants to get to a specific elevator lobby.

"Alright guys. You got about eight badasses headed your way at ten o'clock. They look cartel bred. I'm detecting body armor." Robby warned through their headset.

"I will handle this." Sinus offered as he took hold of the Korean broadsword from his back. "Second unit. On me!"

Sinus took six men and ran ahead of Eliza down the left path. The security guards were all built men who looked strong enough to play professional football. As Robby detected, they were equipped with body armor and extendable metal night sticks with Tasers on the end of them. Sinus sprinted toward the midst of their group and performed an impressive flying crescent kick to knock out the closest man. With their nightsticks drawn, the security guards rushed Sinus and the 18th soldiers but would eventually turn out to be no match for Sinus' skill.

Eliza had not stopped walking since she entered the casino. She just continued in the same powerwalk pace of someone who knew they wouldn't be stopped. The pedestrians watching her stared with intense curiosity, noticing the beauty in her green eyes, the danger exhibited from her mysteriously overwhelming confidence.

With the larger force of 18th soldiers, Eliza led the men down a walkway that overlooked a fancy French cuisine style restaurant theater. Businessmen and mobsters with their overpriced escorts watched with a calm curiosity as a hooded Eliza seemed to stroll down the aisle as if she owned the place. Security guards continued to pop up out of nowhere at which point an individual 18th soldier would take them on in a man-to-man fight while the rest stayed with Eliza.

Whilst walking through the restaurant, Eliza caught sight of a group of underage teenagers by the bar. They were all dressed in high school uniforms, but drinking and smoking casually as if it was their regular hangout spot. One of the girls, a Latino with long black hair and two distinct golden braids coming down between her eyes, seemed the ringleader of the group. Her feisty brown eyes glared at Eliza. The 18th commander's green eyes glared back. The two ladies had never met before, but Eliza had a feeling it wouldn't be the last time she'd see this girl's face.

Upon exiting the restaurant and theater, Eliza and the group entered a large populated arena of the high stakes poker games. She stopped with her hands in her coat pockets to take a look around. Brian pointed over her shoulder to toward the other side of the room. There, she saw her destination, a set of doors that led to an exclusive elevator lobby. This set of doors was locked and required a palm print and keycard for access. Robby was already in the midst of hacking it.

"Hate to break it to you, but there's a bunch of armed assholes in this room. I'm picking up six armed weapon signatures and fifteen guards wearing body armor under their suits." Robby warned through their earpieces.

"We came here half expecting this." Eliza replied calmly.

The poker players were all either corrupt officials, decadent celebrities or mob affiliates. Both security guards and the bodyguards of those mob affiliates were moving in on their position. The guards had no idea what to expect. The poker players thought it was some kind of joke, hired entertainment or something. Meanwhile, Eliza led her men into a large clearing in the center of the room and stopped. She turned to face the group of trained guards who were steadily approaching. She then turned to throw a glance towards Priest Edwin's petrifying blue eyes. The Priest nodded, not needing to hear any orders.

"Fourth unit. On me." Priest said as he pulled out a long golden three section staff that snapped into a long pole. With ten men, Priest Edwin walked casually to greet the guards.

Eliza then took the assault rifles from Brian and Slater and gave them to the two closest 18th soldiers. The two men, Harkins and Ledger, were both in their late 40s, already sprouting white hair. Looking one of them in the eye, Eliza ordered, "Clean these assholes out. They give you any trouble. Shoot them in the nutsacks."

"Yes ma'am." Harkins confirmed in a thick country accent.

Harkins and Ledger rallied the remaining 18th men to start to work on the poker tables. The poker players were initially just watching them with complacent amusement but turned stunned and angry when they found out they had become targets.

"Alright you cocksuckers! Put em hands up! Anyone move and I'll pop you faster than a rattlesnake in a tool shed!" Harkins shouted in a thick country accent.

Priest Edwin and his unit engaged the security guards in intense combat. You could hear the metal ringing vibration as Edwin's long golden staff connected with the back of a man's head. As expected, the celebrities and mobsters all put up a fight instead of submissively handing over their valuables. It was like comparable to watching an old western ballroom brawl that was one-sided. August the 18th was completely dominant. Catching the feed of surveillance cameras through his monitors, even Robby was awestruck by the rambunctious sight. There were chips flying like popcorn, money flying like confetti. Chairs were used as clubs and tables flipped over like dominos. Wine was spilt over hundred thousand dollar dresses and tuxedos and one elderly man broke out into a heart attack right there on the scene. Yes…the toothy amused smile Robby displayed couldn't be contained.

Convinced that her comrades could handle their own, Eliza casually led Brian and Slater through the chaos to reach the set of doors leading into the elevator lobby. She tried to turn the door handle, but it didn't turn. Instead of asking Robby about it, Eliza calmly, yet aggressively, raised a right boot for a brick-breaking shove kick to burst through the door handle. This effectively granted them access to the lobby.

"Damn it, Robby! Where were you with access to the executive elevator lobby?" Slater shouted.

"It was unlocked! You only needed to pull it, dumbass!" Robby barked back. "Get on my level."

"Enough you two. This is crazy." Brian uttered as he threw a judgmental glare Eliza's way.

Guarding the elevator thirty feet down the lobby, there was a pair of Jagata Sentinels. These six foot tall intimidating militarized androids didn't have the humanoid superficial skin, eyeballs or hair that most service androids possessed. They were created and molded from the model stats of a special forces Kosovo soldier since Albania was the nation known to mass produce these products. Their metallic panels and silver armored casings were barely covered by black sheets of cloth that wrapped around their upper and lower body. They were bullet proof, water proof and immune to electrical attacks. For twenty-four hours a day seven days a week, these machines were assigned to stand guard by these elevators armed with just their strength, dexterity and five foot battle axes that were designed and polished with such luster that the sentinels looked just like large ornamental statues on most days.

Initially, Eliza was confused and curious when she approached and laid eyes on them. It wasn't until Brian whipped out his semi-automatic pistol and identified what they were that these machines suddenly detected a malevolent danger and automatically set their systems to engage. The rubber bullets from Brian's gun did nothing to stop the loud metallic clanks from their run. If Eliza didn't rush forward when she did, Brian and Slater would've been hacked down.

Bursting with the speed of a jaguar on the hunt, Eliza dashed low and close to the wall before jumping forward to wrap her legs around the head of the closet Jagata. With its visual sensors blocked, the sentinel began to wobble in a discombobulated stumble. As Eliza tried to pry the Jagata's head off from its body, the Artificial Intelligence of the remaining sentinel thought it would be a good idea to swing its ax at her. Of course, Eliza quickly back-flipped off of that thing and the Jagata was decapitated for her.

With its back turned on the two law enforcement officers, Captains Slater and Wells ran forward to slap C-4 strips the size of business cards on its back. The small fireball explosion caused the sentinel to fly forward towards Eliza. Instead of moving out of the way, Eliza showed a sudden bout of freakish aggression by catching the 600 pound machine by its legs and whipping it down in a powerbomb move onto the floor. The tile shattering impact caused more damage than the C-4 did. And just to make sure it was down for good, Eliza stomped a three inch imprint of her boot into its titanium chest. The wheezing of its internal core powered down.

Slater and Wells saw this and instinctively backed away from her as if she had suddenly become the threat. Eliza wasn't sweating or panting as she pressed the elevator button. She didn't seemed on edge or proud of her achievement at all. She just seemed more disgruntled than anything. As if it was insulting that those simple machines had the audacity to try her. Thus, her eyebrows were lowered over those squinting green eyes as she watched the holographic screen show the lift descending floor by floor.

"Um…damn…well…" Robby whispered.

The elevator doors opened. August the 18th entered. Once the doors were closed, Robby gave the following instructions. "Now press three, five, and the number eight three times. Only the number eight, three times."

Eliza entered the floor codes correctly to get the elevator moving when suddenly two panels in the upper corners of the elevator opened to make way for sentry machine guns. They whipped out so fast with a hard popping metallic pop that even Eliza jumped with fright. But even though the turrets were spinning, no bullets were firing. Eliza, Wells and Slater could hear a soft suppressing cackle through their headsets. Robby had disabled them and forgot to issue a warning. Thus the brief terror on the otherwise intimidating 18th leaders was a comical sight. Slater had balled up his fist and was about to say something before Eliza raised her hand to calm him. Her irritated head nod of understanding was a sign conveying that she planned on having a serious conversation with Robby later.

The only video monitor feed Robby wasn't able to disrupt was a flat screen implanted inside the desk of the executive vice-president's office. This office was wide and spacious enough to fit two bowling lanes against the wall with a twenty-five foot mirror coffee table in the center. The computers, monitors and almost every digital device in this office were using a secure and private wireless connection in which the network was owned exclusively by the Pierce Corporation. Not even the best world-class hackers in the ICSA could disrupt that signal.

The casino's executive vice-president was a tall voluptuous Cuban woman in her mid-40s, the notorious Sofia Monteiro. When Eliza first arrived, Sofia was in the middle of a meeting with her luxury development team. By the time Eliza was walking through the restaurants, she had them sent away and was now in the company of her two trusted assistants and her own personal team of bodyguards. With her sweating palms pressed against the surface of her desk, Sofia watched with anxiety as August the 18th continued to wreak havoc on the craps floor.

Her male assistant, Joaquin, was a gay man in his mid-thirties, always dressed in slimming shiny silks. He was on a desktop computer in the corner, frantically backing up files, documents and account information onto a cloud storage site before deleting them. Lapita was basically a much younger version of Sofia, but clearly lacking the ambition, courage and aggression needed to be Sofia's successor. Since the security systems were breached she pleaded and begged for Sofia to use the secret passage behind the mini-bar to make her escape, but her cries were falling on deaf ears. Leaving the office unattended for three unknown intruders was unthinkable.

"Dios mio…" She snarled as she ran her fingers through her thick brown hair.

She had already notified the police, Kelly Rosetti's family and a high-ranking Pierce official, but she knew they'd never get there in time. She had to force herself to calm down. It wasn't the first time she's been robbed at gunpoint. She had to remind herself who she was.

"Lapita, SHUT UP! Go drink something, you idiot!" She screamed.

The nerve-wrecked Lapita broke down in a corner as if she were just raped and thrown aside. Her puppy-dog eyes of sorrow had no effect on the hardened vice-president. Sofia was not only a cold-blooded murdering book-running genius, she was also a highly influential seductress. On her rise to power starting at the age of sixteen, Monteiro performed the intimate duties of a mistress to a myriad of mob bosses, politicians and judges. No one becomes the vice-president of a half a billion dollar casino with a limited education and no inheritance unless they had the right connections. And Sofia Monteiro scratched the winning lottery ticket when she conceived a child with one of the wealthiest men in the world.

Monteiro's personal team of bodyguards was not on the casino's payroll. The six men team were assigned Black Creek operatives, wearing black dress suits and armed with Uzi submachine guns and sheathed long sabers down by their waists. Without saying a word, they stood alert and diligent around the glass table in the center of the room.

Only one of the six men sat lounging on the brown leather couch in the center of the room. This man wasn't dressed in a black suit or armed with the same weaponry. Sixty percent of Hector Mashima's body was composed of bionic mechanical engineering with cybernetic implants in his quads, thighs, shoulders and arms. He wore a layer of muscular padded thermo-grade prosthetic skin to withstand most sharp edges and blunt force trauma. Thus, he looked like a seven foot Japanese pro wrestler, wearing nothing but black cargo pants and boots with a yakuza tattoo of a koi fish on his back.

"Eliza, can you hear me?" Robby asked.

"Yes. What's up?"

"It's weird. I'm not picking up any heat signatures in the manager's office. I can hear you guys, but if there are any cameras in that office it must be on a shadow network. I'm not sure how it's blocking out the satellites' infrared RSS feeds. I'm sorry. I don't know what you're walking into." Robby warned her.

Despite Robby's disconcerting warning Eliza remained ever dauntless. If she couldn't see…she could still hear and smell. Brian and Slater noticed as she closed her eyes with an intense focus. Eliza could hear the sobbing from Lapita. The typing of Joaquin's keyboard. And the frantic heartbeats from more than four individuals, but it was difficult to pinpoint how many. Sofia Monteiro was surprisingly silent as she contemplated her next move.

"Get Benji on the phone! Now!" Sofia screamed at one of the Black Creek soldiers.

Just as one of the soldiers was reaching for a cell phone in the breast pocket of his jacket, there was a soft chime from the elevator. The Black Creek soldiers heard the chime and extended the stock to adjust the butt of the weapon against their shoulders. The three metal clicks of the adjustable stock were similar to the sound of a loading magazine clip and Eliza heard it all.

Standing in the middle, Eliza used both hands to push Captain Wells and Slater away from her, slamming them into the walls and out of the way of the doorframe. Before the Black Creek soldiers started shooting through the doors, Eliza jumped up with all of her strength to breach through the elevator ceiling using her forearm and elbow to shield her head.

After watching the men open fire on the elevators for close to ten prolonged seconds before finally shouting for them to stop. The doors slid open with a jerking strain with all the bullet holes riddling them. But as soon as there was a large enough gap, Slater and Wells starting popping off shots with their sidearm.

They were able to hit two Black Creek soldiers before the men in suits decided to open fire again and by then, Slater had tossed out a flash grenade. The blinding light and explosive bang stunned everyone in the room. The five seconds of vision and hearing impairment was all Eliza needed to drop from the ceiling, swing back in and get to work.

Unleashing Ivy from its sheath, she quickly dispatched two men by slitting their throats. She stabbed a third through his sternum and was about to hack at a fourth before Mashima caught her arm in mid-swing and slung her across the room like a ragdoll. Eliza dropped to the floor with a hard thud just two feet from Lapita's position. It was incredible. The frightened assistant's fears were only exacerbated when she saw the hooded figure rise to one knee so quickly, still clutching a blood soaked sword in hand. And as Mashima flipped over the couch that was in his way to get to her, Lapita started to lose her mind, erupting in a seizure and releasing a hair-raising scream that was almost as loud as the flash grenade.

With two hands, the monstrous Mashima grabbed Eliza off the ground by her neck and shoved her head back into the wall. But for some reason, the cyborg kept getting distracted by Lapita's screaming. Because Lapita kept screaming, over and over again one breath after another like a possessed woman about to be crucified.

Through the midst of Slater and Wells' firefight with the remaining two Black Creek soldiers, two more shots rang out. Sofia had just used her personalized Glock 42 to pacify Lapita for good. But she didn't stop there. The casino executive boldly walked around her desk to get a better shot at Eliza. Firing careless, she ended up clipping Mashima's left forearm. The weakened grip was just was she needed to twist the wounded arm.

His pain receptors must've been shut off because Mashima showed no reaction from the bullet wound or the fact that one of his arms was now dangling like rope. Just an angry grimace that seemed to say, "Now you've done it". With his good right arm, he tried to swing at Eliza but ended up hitting nothing but plaster. Eliza easily dodged the swing and drove the tip of her sword through his abdomen. With her strength and the razor sharp edge of her blade, it wasn't hard to carve through layers of processing wiring, sheet metal and prosthetic skin. Mashima dropped to the ground with a rainbow colored swirl of water and oil oozing out of his mutilated body.

Realizing she was out of bullets, Sofia rushed back to her desk to retrieve another clip. But by then, Slater and Wells had finished off their opponents. Both ended up having to slay their Black Creek opponents who wouldn't stay down for the count. Slater had one of the Black Creek's Uzis and clipped the back of Sofia's thigh as she ran, causing her to fall and hit the corner of her desk with her shoulder.

"NOO!!!" Joaquin shouted.

The flamboyant assistant had remained in cover, squatting beside the desktop computer during the fire fight. But upon seeing his benefactor fall with such a sympathy-inducing whimper, he gathered the courage to take a dead bodyguard's saber and rush on the offensive. Captain Wells easily moved forward while Joaquin's sword was foolishly raised too high. With a jerking hip toss, he flipped the assistant onto the ground and finished him with a stern punch to the mandible.

Back on the casino floors, the battles were winding down. Most of the 18th members were finished fighting security guards and robbing the high rollers and were now trashing the place by knocking over tables, smashing windows while letting civilians retreat. Sinus and Priest, however, were still smashing faces in and delivering cuts in the poker room. Whoever wanted it, the two of them stepped up to deliver. They seemed to revel in it. They couldn't get enough of it. They were blood brothers born.

"Alright guys wrap it up." Robby warned through their headsets. "We got less than two minutes before SWAT rolls through. Dispatch think there's some kind of syndicate dispute going on so they're gonna come in bangin and shankin."

Eliza heard the warning as she approached the hobbling Sofia Monteiro. "Tell the boys to pack up and fall out. If we're not down stairs in ninety seconds then, leave without us." Eliza said.

"Who are you? Huh? Don't you know who I am? Who I work for?" Sofia growled in a heated sweat as she finally managed to get behind her desk.

She started to fumble through the drawers in search for something, anything. And as Slater raised his sidearm to take another shot, Eliza raised his hand to him to stop him. She wanted to see what Sofia would do.

"Fucking cabron…Wearing masks won't save you. There's nowhere to hide in this city. Huh! Take off that fucking mask, you spineless guero! Show me you got some balls!" Sofia shouted.

She finally managed to find a ceremonial two-foot Spanish rapier that was hanging on hooks just under the top panel of her desk. Eliza's green eyes scanned the woman. She sensed anxiety in Sofia's gaze…a sense of hopelessness, yet a determination to die standing on her own two feet. No regrets. No repentance. She didn't give a damn about whether she was right or wrong. And she didn't think twice about shooting her own assistant.

Eliza removed her hood and wiped the sweat off of her head with the back on her hand. That was when an insulting anger took over Sofia. Eliza was a fellow female, blonde, young and beautiful. Each second that passed with Eliza staring at her like she was her superior only fueled the rage. With a teeth-clenching grunt, Sofia fought through the pain in her legs to run for Eliza and lunged the sword tip aimed between the eyes.

Quicker than the snap of a mousetrap, Eliza easily dashed forward and grabbed her sword wielding wrist to raise the blade from doing any harm. Sofia tried in vain to pull her arm away, but it was like she was caught in cement.

"Spanish rapier. Funny. I used to have one of those. Way back when I didn't know any better." Eliza told her.

Even with Eliza's mask on, you could tell she was smiling from her squinting eyes. Just as Sofia tried to slap her, Eliza raised Ivy to slice through the forearm she was holding. Drizzling blood spilled on the floor as Sofia shrieked in pain. It was then that she finally began to show the remorse and regret that Eliza was pursuing. Wailing in a strained groan, Sofia stumbled backwards toward the wall as tears and agony stretched down her face. Slater and Wells approached, both feeling concern and sympathy toward the attractive female who was shaking her head no as if she was being asked a thousand questions at once.

Eliza showed no sympathy. No mercy. With Ivy clenched in hand, she approached the gabbling woman.

"Eliza..." Wells whispered.

"Quiet!" Eliza snapped.

Sofia started to breathe hard, hugging her severed throbbing arm with her back against the wall. But when Eliza walked to stand over her, she gradually chuckled into an insane laugh. "I can't be killed. I can't die. Hahaha... I snap my fingers and other people die. You get it? Do you? You understand me you stupid little girl?" She snarled with a half-assed attempt to spit.

"Last month you set up an underground street fight with some middle school girls. Six of those girls died. Another one, Amanda Haman, died two days later from brain damage, you rat-faced cancer." Eliza told her.

Sofia laughed harder. "This is why you're doing this? For school girls? I am Sofia Monteiro! I can persuade entire schools to host a fucking kumite for my own personal amusement. Whores, all of them. In the world we live in, women either serve or be served. And I choose to be served."

"Don't say it, Liz. Too easy…And cheesy." Robby sarcastically interjected.

"Hey! Can you bastards stop saying my name so loosely?" Eliza stressed.

"Yeah, we probably should've made up some code names…Brian!" Robby said.

"You guys, I'm pretty sure SWAT is downstairs. Right now." Brian Wells interjected.

"Get on with it!" Slater barked.

Eliza raised her blood drenched katana and aimed it for Sofia's throat as the wounded animal gave another half-assed spit attempt. "The godfather himself will hear of this."

"Yeah. Well…That's kind of the point." Eliza said in a cheerful tone. Without further ado, Eliza gave a quick thrust to stick her sword through the center of Sofia's throat.

…

Inspector Gazi arrived on the scene an hour after Sofia's death. The incident drew the attention of almost every news broadcast station in the country. Hundreds of videos from the raid were posted on dozens of social media sites. Most college students had watched what happened before the proper authorities did. Walking onto the blackjack floor, Gazi bore witness to the path of destruction that was caused in a little under eight minutes. No slot machine was without a busted screen. No roulette and blackjack table stood without shredded felt. Signs were hanging on by a thread. Employees were distraught in their statements. And there was blood, severed limbs and injured bodies scattered about.

All eight casualties were dealt by Eliza with only one security guard surviving her ninja star to the throat. There were sixty-two injured victims suffering from a range of fractured bones, dislocated joints, ruptured organs or blunt force trauma. Eight men were losing blood at a rapid rate from open sword wounds and had to be airlifted to the nearest hospitals. Some of the injured were still on the floor, being questioned by investigators. As expected, most of the mob affiliates in the high stakes poker room refrained from cooperating with the police. Only their escorts and civilian guests gave exaggerated stories of what happened.

"I was just checking in with my husband!" One elderly woman from Arkansas began with a reporter. "Then all I heard was cars honking. And I turned around. And I saw this one guy coming out of one of those trucks throwing knives. And I screamed. I wasn't sure if they were dead or not, but there was blood everywhere. It was horrible!"

"Yeah, there was this Asian guy." A middle-aged man with a country accent said to another reporter. "Here I was tryin ma luck at the Triple Golden Aces slots and all I see is this Asian dude come flyin through the air, kicking and swinging his sword like he was a goddamn monkey on the stuff man! Man, I ain't never seen nothin like it!"

"All I know is that I was $52,000 strong." A large man with an Italian accent began with dramatic hand gestures. "Then these green fruity faggets stroll in here and kick everyone out. I tell you what! I plan to sue this place ten times what I'm owed. One of them hit me! I lost a tooth. See!" The Italian said, pulling back on his cheeks to show a missing molar.

Inspector Detective Gazi didn't know what to make of it. From the quick reports he received from deputies on the scene, Gazi's first assumption was that it was a daring raid from a new gang trying to create a name for themselves. But to hit one of the most lucrative casinos in the country, attacking mobsters and politicians alike...it was too bold for some simple street crew.

Nothing could've prepared him for the carnage that awaited him in the executive vice-president's office. The first responders were given explicit orders to leave the bodies as is until the detectives arrived. So they took photos and Joaquin's statements as CSI combed the room for physical evidence.

Lapita's eyes were wide open with a gashing bullet wound just above her right ear. Mashima's body was still decaying in oil and water with a single footprint left by someone stepping over him. Five dead men were scattered on the floor in a pool of their own blood. A forensic team was already on the scene along with Detective Inspectors Walsh and Di Mare. Both inspectors wore grim expressions as they examined the bodies and tried to piece how the assailant entered and killed the supposedly well-trained Black Creek soldiers. When Gazi entered, no one said anything to him. All you could hear were the continued calls from deputies over the radio, and Joaquin dramatically refusing to say anything without his attorney present. The Inspectors simply gestured for Gazi to go look in the corner of the large office.

Gazi maneuvered his way over the scattered carcasses, cringing at the blood-smeared prints all over the round mirror coffee table in the center of the room. When he approached the corner of the office and removed a small bar towel that covered Sofia's face, he was completely beside himself with disgust. Her severed right hand was lying idle seven feet away. She had a hole in her throat the size of a nickel. A stream of blood had poured over her breast and came down to the navel of her dress. Her eyes were staring down with a crusted trail of dried tears running down her cheeks. There was a sharp pattern of blood spray on the floor in front of her from whence Eliza yanked her sword out of her throat.

Gazi shook his head with sadness and swallowed hard. "This isn't good."

"Gazi…" Inspector Walsh called over.

Inspectors Walsh and Di Mare were standing on the other side of the room by the elevators. There was a young woman with them. She was of mixed Cuban-Caucasian descent, still in high school. With olive colored skin, the stunning young woman had feisty brown eyes and long straight black hair with two distinct golden braids coming down between her eyes. And down by her side there was a four-month-old baby Bengal tiger on a leash. It was a gift from her father for turning seventeen two months earlier. Gazi approached.

"Inspector Gazi. This is Almarylis Monteiro. Sofia's daughter." Di Mare introduced.

"Inspector Di Mare. There are several board executives down here demanding to come up." A female officer reported through his radio piece. "Should I let them up or…"

"No! No. I'll be right down, deputy." Di Mare instructed as he pressed the elevator button. "Alright fellas. I gotta go handle the hounds."

"Good luck." Walsh wished as Di Mare stepped onto the elevator.

Gazi stood with a sincere expression. He had no idea what to say, or where to even start in expressing his condolences. Alma stared with a stoic gaze, chewing her gum and popping it out loud as if she had some place to be. She couldn't see her mother's body from her position but she knew it was over there in the corner.

"Perhaps we should speak elsewhere?" Gazi suggested.

"It's fine. I've seen more bloodshed to last me three lifetimes." Alma said in mature tone that held little to no Latino accent.

"My mother was a ruthless cunt, but she didn't deserve this. I was having drinks with some of my girlfriends down in the bar when I saw em coming."

"Most of the high rollers aren't saying anything. The cameras have all been hacked into. All of the surveillance footage has been destroyed. Ms. Monteiro, if you could help us out with a description. Anything at all would be helpful." Said Inspector Walsh.

Alma casually took a cigarette out of her jacket pocket while looking down at the tiger. The small tiger was sitting next to her fur boots as it pawed at a long cell phone charm that dangled out of Alma's skirt pocket. The teenage heiress took a long puff of the cigarette and folded her arms.

"Pollen, stop that. You'll rip it." Alma told the cub.

Her eyes then shifted up to Gazi, in particular the scar under his right eye. It was a gaze filled with cynicism and doubt. Gazi was gradually coming to the conclusion that Alma was no normal teenage girl. When she said that she'd seen her share of bloodshed, she wasn't lying. No doubt Alma had about as much faith in the police department as a relative would in their dope fiend cousin.

Walsh continued to insist. "We know that they were all wearing green. Some were carrying automatic weapons, Tasers, swords. I think one said they saw a golden staff. Except they weren't shooting live rounds, but rubber bullets."

"Rubber bullets?" Gazi questioned.

"Well…obviously the ones in here were by live 9 mm rounds. But the assault rifles that tore through the slot machines were rubber bullets." Walsh told him.

"So what? They're broke? Or was it never their intention to kill innocents? Sounds very courteous of gang trying to build their reputations. Maybe this is a case of homicide, and all that other nonsense was just a diversion."

"Come on Gazi…" Walsh said. "It's a bit grand for a diversion, isn't it? You can put this up with that plane that crashed down in Clearwater last August. Now what do we got? Huh? A group of about forty to fifty individuals. All grown men, ranging from late twenties to early forties."

"They weren't all men." Alma pointed out.

The room turned silent. Both of inspectors and even some men and women on the forensics team stopped what they were doing to give Alma their attention.

"Ms. Monteiro, I have to ask. How do you know that?" Gazi questioned with his hands on his hips.

"I told you." Alma snapped with an attitude. "I was having drinks with my girls in the bar when I saw them coming. They were all following this tall white bitch. She wore this long green trench coat with a hood like something out of dragon tales or some shit."

"And you *know* she was a woman?" Walsh asked for confirmation.

"All the coats in the world couldn't hide those puppies. All prim and perky. And I think I saw some of her hair." Alma added.

"That's great. What color was she?" Walsh asked.

Alma rolled her eyes. "Look, I told you! She was a white girl. With blond hair. And green eyes."

<u>Chapter 15 – Strike Two: Breaking the Bank</u>

On a Tuesday night of mid-October, a heavy downpour of freezing rain fell upon the entire city. The conditions made the streets eerily desolate and abandoned for it being downtown Tampa. The few cars that commuted the roads drove at a slow lazy pace. The Halo lights seemed faint. The homeless took to the shelters indoors, and even the police on patrol took naps in their cars or caught up on their recent mystery subscriptions. Even so…as per usual…Tampa was never without someone going against the grain.

Frank Parcell was a detective working the undercover beat for going on six years straight out of the academy. He was a rough looking skinny figure, approaching 30, with pale skin, short black hair, and a rugged mustache goatee. On such a horrid day, Parcell was walking on the sidewalk leading up to the main Tampa Metropolitan Police Department. Bundled in a thick brown raincoat and a scarf that wrapped around most of his face, Parcell held up an umbrella for the rain. In his lonely stroll he was contemplating, reminiscing about the last six years.

"To protect and serve…." Parcell thought to himself. "That concepts a joke during this day in age. We know who the criminals are out there. We know their faces. We even know where to find them. But all these goddamn lawyers and their twists and turns. Loopholes and special clauses. Evidence…it's like the system was amended in place to provide a constant need for our services. For us to catch em, then let them go. Only so they can commit the same crime and have us catch them again. Is that really the case? To keep the need for police to remain at an all-time high. If it weren't for local law enforcement positions, all of us from the border wars would be out of the job. But would that really be a problem?"

"For years now, it seems like the Imperial government has just been letting the syndicate grow. As if the nation somehow benefits from the backhanded murders and sudden corporate takeovers that the media only makes obvious light mention of. Now we got this vigilante group all decked out in green, just massacring and taking out whoever the hell. The fuck is this world coming to?" He continued to ponder.

Parcell now stood with his hands in his pockets in front of the ten-foot bronze statue of lady justice that was erected in front of the TMPD building. A sigil and symbol of righteousness. Parcell looked up to it, almost teary eyed from a combination of hopelessness and the numbing cold. Disheartened and frustrated, Parcell shook his head.

"There's got to be more to life than this. There has got to be something more I can do!" Parcell said aloud to himself.

He looked to his right. There were a few cars parked on the street, but no souls. He looked to his left. Traffic was scarce at the nearby intersection. After taking in a deep breath, he started on his way for the pay phone on the street corner. The rain was beginning to soak into his boots. The rain on the sidewalk was beginning to freeze into ice. Upon opening the door to the phone booth, he found an elderly man wrapped in a thick warn-out comforter. The homeless man instantly woke up, startled with fright.

Parcell nodded at the homeless man sympathetically. "Give me five minutes and you can have it back. Don't worry. I won't mess with your blanket. No need in taking it out and getting it all soggy and what not."

The homeless man nodded cautiously before grabbing onto handles to climb up to a stand. Parcell helped him. Before exiting the booth, he gave the man his umbrella. Then, Parcell closed the door and waited till the homeless man was a good distance away. After making sure his end was clear, Parcell placed a call using a prepaid card to make the payment.

In a dimly lit suite on the thirty-second floor of the luxurious Pierce Hotel, Miguel Lobos was lounging back in a love seat while an exclusive high-priced prostitute slowly unbuttoned his finely starched shirt, tenderly kissing his well-toned chest down to his navel. Lobos was an American born descendant of a wealthy Mexican family. He was in his mid-50s, but blessed with extremely good looks and an impressive physique that made him appear to be in his mid-30s. His short silver tipped black hair was combed back with a gel that made his hair look like steel. He had a rich tan complexion but his most notable features were his pair of small squinting distinct baby-blue eyes.

This man was the Deputy Superintendent in charge of running the Criminal Enterprise Division of TMPD. He was just one notch below the Police Commissioner, and was also the man both Di Mare and Walsh answered to when things went sour, which was often. This was the division that handled specialized criminal activity such as money laundering, gang violence, organized crime and cartel enterprise. Given the danger and international spread of such crimes, the CE division often worked hand in hand with Interpol, the Port Authority and the American Imperial Bureau of Investigation. That being said, Superintendent Lobos was a powerful man with powerful connections. The fact that he's stayed in his position for close to a decade given the rise of homicides, abduction and terrorism is a powerful message in of itself.

Lobos' personal cell phone was ringing. While he knew to expect the call, he was still preoccupied in the heat of the moment. He turned down the smooth jazz that played from the stereo next to the mini bar. The woman whispered something in his ear. And even though Lobos barely understand a single Arabic word she spoke, he still smiled and gestured for her to go get in the bed with a pat on the ass.

Lobos leaned over toward the end table and picked up his phone to answer it. "I do hope this is important." Lobos said as he massaged his forehead.

"Sir. It's as I've been saying all along." Parcell began on the other end of the line. "The Capo, Simon Casker, is planning to make his move on Thursday the 22nd. He hasn't told us what time. But I was there in person when Noah Rosenberg gave him the order."

Lobos reached for his glass of cognac and shook the cubes. "Go on..."

"I'm telling you, these guys are going to hit the Tampa Metropolitan Bank and they don't plan on leaving without executing at least six civilians. Noah said it's an order handed down from up top. Something about the bank manager not paying dividends. But it was an *order*. He didn't say from whom, but there are only two people who can give him an order and that's his brother Bosco or…Sir. We're talking about the head of the Jewish mafia here. Maybe even the Pierce themselves."

Lobos stood up, wide-eyed with concern. "Whoa! Hey, hey, hey! What the hell are you thinking? Are you using a landline? This phone conversation can be intercepted. Retraced! You're putting your life on the line here."

"It's not like that sir. I'm using a disrupter on my end. No one but you can hear my voice and vice versa." Parcell lied intentionally.

There was a heavy sigh on Lobos' end. "Did Noah say, Pierce? Did they mention anyone from the Pierce Corporation at all?"

"Well, no sir. But it's kind of obvious. I mean, why else…"

"Give me the facts, detective." Lobos ordered.

"Verbatim, Noah Rosenberg said our actions should be seen as retaliation toward this new group, pulling off that raid on the casino a couple of weeks ago. Now, I'm not sure why killing six civilians has anything to do with the casino raid. But that's what the jerkoff said." Parcell told him, slightly letting his frustrations show.

Lobos pondered deeply. "What do you know of this new group?" He asked.

The pounding rain made it difficult for Parcell to hear, but he wore a puzzled look due to Lobos' question. "Sir? I don't know much about this new group. Sir! With all due respect, I think you're missing the point. They plan to rob the bank as a cover to intentionally execute six innocent civilians!"

Lobos stood up in his hotel suite and stormed away from the prostitute's position. "No. You don't understand, detective! Ever since that incident, every branch of law enforcement in the state has been pulling out all stops for any and all information about this new group of green bandits. As superintendent, all rivers of boiling bullshit run down to me. So why don't you leave the thinking to me, eh."

Parcell sighed. "What do you want me to do, sir?"

"I know this might be difficult to swallow. But I need you to just go along and do whatever they ask of you." Lobos told him.

Parcell planted his forehead against the cold glass and banged it softly twice. He didn't respond. He couldn't. So Lobos continued. "Look. You're an undercover cop. If the lot of you get cuffed, they won't come after you for your involvement. I'll back you up. Just stick with it, and go along with the robbery. Look. I handpicked you straight out of the academy. I saw potential in you and gave you the rank of detective when most uniforms go their entire lives straining their ankles to reach your rank. Trust me, son."

Upon hearing those words, Parcell finally lost the last remaining ounce of respect that he had for his commanding officer and the idea of even possessing a badge. Almost as if his mind was literally blown, Parcell simply hung up the phone and stared at it, realizing that the only person on earth who knew he was a cop just signed off on the death warrants of six husbands, six wives, six daughters, six sons. He had a twenty that he was planning to spend on at the bar. He bent down to tuck the bill within the comforter that was bundled on the floor at his feet. The homeless man in the rain turned at the sound of metal clanking from the booth door opening. Without saying a word, Parcell took back his umbrella and made on his way down the wet, icy sidewalk.

...

Robby arrived at the 18th Headquarters around noon the next day. There were close to fifteen members there. Most had only just stopped by briefly to check a large bulletin monitor that they were required to check for updates on meetings and assignments. In the communications section, two former Naval Intelligence operatives named Austin and Stephen were working on Robby's personal desktop computer. There were three other computer stations set up. But they were on Robby's. Both wearing headphones and both were looking at the same monitor as if one was getting the opinion of the other. As expected, Robby was a tad bit irritated.

He approached the two while shaking his head and biting his lower lip. After briefly standing there staring wide-eyed at them with a lack of greeting, he swung his backpack against the workstation only hard enough to get their attention. "Stephen. Austin. Now I know you guys heard me the last time I told you. Haha… I know because I was shouting. Stay off of this computer. You got three other PCs, right over here."

Stephen and Austin ignored him, both listening intensively to something being played through their headphones. Robby stared at them with a blank face, his eyebrows comically rising on their own. As was his temper. While Stephen and Austin were trained field operatives, they were still smaller than Robby and didn't appear as intimidating as some of the other members.

Robby reached for Stephen's headphones. "Hey douche! I know you hear me." He shouted.

Austin grabbed Robby by the wrist to stop him and sternly handed him another pair of headphones that was hooked into the same computer. A snarl quickly formed and disappeared as Robby stared at the headphones. He finally snatched them up and walked around the desk so he could see the monitors. Stephen pressed a hotkey on the keyboard to start the recording from the beginning. As he listened, Robby's jaw lowered at the same time as his eyebrows. He couldn't believe it. It was the recording of Parcell and Superintendent Lobos' phone conversation. After they finished listening, Austin and Stephen looked up to give Robby a blatant stare.

"Maybe if you installed the keyword recognition software on all the computers we wouldn't have to use yours." Austin told him.

"He's just afraid his position here will be obsolete since we can do everything that he can do. He'll be useless." Stephen added as he stood up and shouldered past Robby.

Robby swallowed their words with a grain of salt, mostly because he knew they were right. But that didn't stop him from showing an obscene gesture with his middle finger. He didn't just flash the middle finger, but he held it up just inches away from their faces and let it linger. Once satisfied, he took out his cell phone and placed a call to Eliza.

"Hey…Yeah I'm here. Listen. I think we need to call an emergency meeting today as soon as possible with all the captains. Yeah, Ham and Cheese found something. It's kind of messed up, man." Robby told her.

After finishing his brief conversation with Eliza, Robby turned around to see Austin and Stephen whipping up their coats and exiting out the front entrance. Feeling slightly ashamed, Robby clawed off his padded coat and took the time to install every piece of software that he owned or stole to every computer in the building. This process filled up the four hours it took for the captains and Eliza to arrive with several other 18th members who thought of themselves as strategists.

They held the meeting in the upstairs loft that was Eliza's office. Her office was furnished with a black leather sofa set, a large polished desk, and a monitor that was used to hook up wirelessly to any computer. She always took off her green-leaved katana sword, Ivy, to set on a placeholder on the edge of the desk. She also had three custom-made green hooded overcoats hanging on one side of the office.

In the cabinet counters and glass cases, Eliza displayed an assortment of weapons she mastered, along with a small collection of artistic facemasks and fingerless weightlifting gloves that she wore out in the field. All of the additional furniture and updated equipment was paid for by the money stolen from the casino raid weeks earlier. Brian Wells was put in charge of the business account using one of his aliases.

Sinus, Slater, Brian, Priest Edwin and three other August the 18th members were all either standing around or sitting down on the couch set that was in front of Eliza's desk. All of them, with the exception of Sinus, were dressed in professional working class uniforms as if they had just gotten off from their day jobs. Robby walked up the stairs into the office and handed them all a printed transcript of the phone conversation. Parcell and Lobos' names were never mentioned in the recording so instead they were labeled subjects "A" and "B" respectively.

Eliza, who had just finished cramming her head with twenty-two pages of Biometry notes, honestly didn't feel like reading two more. "What is this, Robby? Just come out and say it. This is kind of short notice so I'm sure everyone wants to just…"

"I think there's gonna be a bank robbery tomorrow. During the course of which, six people will be randomly targeted and executed." Robby told them.

"What?" Slater asked in astonishment.

"Just read it, man." Robby told him in earnest.

"Do we know who these people are?" Priest Edwin asked after briefly skimming over the pages.

Robby walked to the wall behind Eliza and turned on a large flat-screen monitor mounted on the wall. His personal laptop was already sitting on her desk. It was synched with the screen. It showed an academy photo of Parcell and his profile.

"I think I know who Subject A is, but it's just a hunch. Subject B identified him as an undercover cop with the Rosenberg Association. He said he became a detective straight out of the academy. Which made things way too easy because out of the sixty-two encrypted undercover files, there's only one detective who doesn't have single a collar to his name. This guy, Joakim Kravitz, was supposedly arrested six years ago as a part of an electronics heist in Tallahassee. It's not hard evidence of course, but it seems his boss Simon Casker is a lieutenant under Noah Rosenberg. Joakim Kravitz's real name is Frank Parcell." Robby explained.

Slater shook his head. "Our cyber security department ain't worth a damn if a friggin college student can find this shit out about our undercover cops!"

"Seems *this* cop is in an awkward position." Brian said, steering the conversation back on track.

Eliza had just finished reading the transcript. While everyone seemed to care about Parcell's position, Eliza's mind was focused on the cold-hearted public official who would let six civilians die. She turned to look at Robby. "If we know who he is, then how hard is it to find out Subject B?"

Slater spoke up to answers. "Nah, darlin. It ain't that easy. Even if his file showed which pay grade he reported to, which it wouldn't, it's not unusual for the undercover to speak with several contacts from upstairs."

"Yeah, but this man said he made him a detective straight out of the academy. Like, only a handful of authority figures can do that, right?"

Eliza's inquiry silenced the room. It was a disconcerting thought that no one knew the answer to.

"Do you think Gazi could know?" Robby asked Eliza.

Eliza squinted her eyes and crossed her arms. "Just because he hasn't had significant progress with the syndicate doesn't mean he's not annoyingly perceptive. I've known the man since I was little and the first thing I picked up on is that Gazi likes to throw things back in your face. If I even asked as innocently and politely as I possibly could, Gazi would remember the question and get to the bottom of every possible reason as to why I would ask. Just to be clear, you guys, I have no doubt that eventually Gazi will find out who I am and what we're doing here. But before he does, I want to be in a position where there wouldn't be much he could do about it."

"So…even if he does know, you don't want to ask him about it." Robby concluded.

"Yeah." Eliza answered.

"Yeah." Robby repeated. Eliza playfully back-handed his arm. Slater rolled his eyes at the college students.

"Why don't we just investigate all of the big wigs? They're all probably just as dirty as this one anyway." Ryan, one of the strategic 18th guest members suggested.

"Nah, that kind of investigation will take years, Ryan." Slater told responded.

Brian was still examining the transcripts closely as the chatter continued on around him. Something about the phone numbers stood out. "I'm assuming you tried both numbers and did a search for their IDs." Brian asked Robby.

Robby nodded. "Yeah. Subject A, I mean, Frank Parcell called from a pay phone outside the main department last night a quarter past midnight. He even lied about it being secured. I think he wanted someone to intercept it."

"What do we know about Noah Rosenberg? Is he really as high up in the food chain as the cop says?" Eliza asked.

"Oh yeah. I have his dossier over here. Let me pull it up." Robby said. From his laptop, he then clicked on a file to show a profile of Noah's through the projector.

The profile revealed that Noah Rosenberg was a convicted murderer, entering his first stint at the Olympus Supermax Prison at the age of 23. Despite witnesses disappearing in his court cases, there was still an honest judge with the heart to sentence him to jail time. The judge's efforts would go in vain however, because Noah was busted out of prison by an unknown paramilitary group while he was being transported to another prison. The judge himself was found several weeks later in the belly of an anaconda. He was subdued by a paralyzing pathogen, tied up, and tossed into an anaconda's cage. The story was sensationalized thoroughly, effectively sending a chilling message to other judges across the nation.

Over the span of two decades, Noah would undergo hundreds of arrests including thirty-two counts of murder, seventeen racketeering charges and eighty-two counts of extortion, all of which never stuck due to a miraculous loss or tampering of evidence. That…and a nervous jury of his peers. After receiving fingerprint implants and facial reconstructive surgery, it became more difficult to identify him as Noah Rosenberg. But the person most suspected of being Noah was a man named Greg Sedway. Sedway owned a successful shipping company in east Tampa, a port in McKay Bay.

"I know most of us are acquainted with most of the top tier factions in the city. The Rosenberg Associate, the Barreira Cartel, the Winter Family of St. Pete, the Kaze-Gumi, etcetera, etcetera. All of them answer to Bosco Rosenberg, aka Boss Rosenberg. With Noah being his only brother, you can bet that he has some pull calling the shots. To put it lightly, if Boss Rosenberg is the king then Noah is his most trusted general. His second-in-command, so to speak. Noah hasn't stepped foot in a courtroom since 2201, and since then he hasn't been seen publically. But he is still wanted for questioning and he's supposedly a fugitive because he hasn't reported to his parole officer in six years. The man suspected of being Noah, is a shipping magnate named Greg Sedway." Robby told them.

"Yeah, I've see his billboards. Obnoxious as hell." One 18th member said.

"Not the best way to lay low." Another added.

"I don't understand. If the police have a good idea of who he is, then why haven't they launched an investigation to get him?" Eliza asked.

"Money, babydoll. Cops are either paid off or not paid enough to risk their lives. Not when there's a whole recorded precedence officers who have lost their lives in that pursuit." Slater told her.

"Let me hear the call." Brian requested of Robby.

"Oh sure. Let me play it from here." Robby said, using his laptop to pull up the sound recording.

As the group listened to the sound recording, all were disgusted with the laid back tone of Subject B. The thought of a corrupt cop compelled Eliza to turn her attention to the picture frame on the corner of her desk. It was the same photo she of her and her father that she brought with her to Korea four years ago.

Then…through the polished wooden desk and the glass covering on top of it, Eliza noticed a reflection. It was a reflection of the ever silent and mysterious Sinus. His arms were folded as he stood leaning with his back against the wall in front of Eliza's desk. His expression was different from the other members. While everyone else strained to detect any clues in the tone of the voices, Sinus seemed as if he recognized the voice and harbored a deep grudge against it.

Impulsively, Eliza twirled a finger through a curly strain of blond hair over her right ear. Her eyes were entranced on Sinus. She needed to know what he was thinking. The enigma was almost a turn-on for her but she maintained a professional front. After watching Sinus' motionless stare for nearly a minute, Eliza leaned over and pressed the space bar on Robby's computer to stop the recording. Everyone looked over and noticed that Eliza's eyes were on Sinus. Even Sinus didn't realize he was being watched until five seconds went by.

"Sinus... I know we all have our various backgrounds and come from some of the deep and darkest places. But I think the only time I've heard you speak was to say "thank you" when you were given a captain's position. Is there anything you'd like to contribute?" Eliza asked politely.

Sinus unfolded his arms and stood up straight, slightly shy and nervous with the attention that he wasn't used to receiving. "Um…yes." Sinus said in a low tone. "That second voice. I believe I have heard it before."

"Where?" Priest Edwin asked him.

"A long time ago, when I was still a child." Sinus told them.

Everyone waited for him to follow up. But he didn't. It wasn't until Eliza smirked while using her hand to beckon him that he nodded and continued.

"I and my older brother were being smuggled into the country by Caribbean pirates. If I am correct and that voice is the same. Um…That man…he was…how do you say…my benefactor. He took me and my brother and enrolled us into an orphanage in St. Petersburg. Over the years, he'd come back and check on me and my brother. And finally one day, he took my older brother and left me. Alone."

No one thought Sinus was lying. But almost everyone suspected he was intentionally hiding something. Priest in particular, believed Sinus was a hardened fighter but with a pure soul. He refused to believe Sinus had some talent for being deceptive. While Brian, Priest, and Eliza tried to make sense of what was just revealed and how the man he was describing could've fit into the equation, both Robby and Slater reserved their doubts about Sinus. The dark silent types are always annoying to those who prefer to speak their minds.

"What's your real name, Sinus?" Slater suddenly demanded to know.

Sinus caught onto his tone and didn't like it.

"Hey. I said what's your fucking name, Robin Hood! I know you speak English, asshole." Slater barked as he stood up and started for Sinus.

Priest Edwin palmed Slater's chest to stop his advance. Eliza thoroughly examined Sinus. Nothing about him seemed corrupt or treacherous. Slater's question seemed harmless, albeit rude in tone. She wondered why Sinus was holding back so much.

"Can you at least tell us the name of the man you're talking about?" Robby asked.

Sinus shook his head no. "Everyone just called him Diablo de ojos Azules."

"The Blue-Eyed Devil?" Brian asked.

"That's right." Sinus confirmed.

"You heard of him?" Slater asked Brian.

Brian nodded with a smirk. "Well. That makes sense. About nine years ago, my wife was investigating a group of house representatives she suspected of financing a group of Surinamese organ traffickers. When they were arrested they kept calling one of their contacts, the Blue-Eyed Devil. They never met with him directly, but mentioned he was someone who pulled the strings. Now, I know this is just a hunch and that we should tread lightly before making any moves, but there's only one high ranking official with this kind of pull with distinct noticeable blue eyes."

"Once the head of the Gang Penetration Division, he's now the Deputy Superintendent of the Criminal Enterprise Division. Miguel Lobos." Brian told them.

Robby and Slater both stood stunned. "No way! I know Superintendent Lobos. Back when he was an inspector he was the one man who campaigned alongside your father when Detective Emil first came up with his theories about Isaac Pierce being some kind of kingpin." Slater declared.

"I know him too." Another 18th member spoke up. "He was the first to arrest Mayor McLaughlin when he was implicated in selling classified itineraries of other governmental officials to domestic terrorists factions. He put his reputation on the line. If he was dirty he wouldn't have stuck his neck out to do that. Not without risking exposure to his own ops."

"Yeah I hear you, but the evidence against McLaughlin was overwhelming. He didn't stretch his neck out there that far." Brian told them.

"I have heard rumors." Priest Edwin contributed. "Lobos does come from an influential Mexican family. I heard that he was once an extreme Nationalist who even has experience in the UNCA's Delta Forces. Not to mention he's relatively young for a superintendent position. He seems to have made all the right moves."

"When I first saw the Blue-Eyed Devil. He was dressed like a soldier." Sinus said, piggy-backing off of Priest Edwin's information.

54

"Robby, pull up a photo of him." Eliza instructed.

Robby went onto the most popular search engine and typed in Miguel Lobos' name. His image appeared above links to several websites dedicated to him. Sinus squinted his already naturally small eyes at the screen. "That's him alright. He's the man that took my brother."

"Get the fuck out. Lobos doesn't wear a mask like the rest of us. If silent knight over here can finger him so easily, why hasn't anyone else step forward?" Slater asked with skepticism.

"Because the rest of "us" is dead!" Sinus shouted, raising his voice for the first time ever and silencing the room. "I only barely escaped with my life."

Eliza closed her eyes and deliberated with her fingers straining through her front bangs. "Gazi…can you really be this blind?" She thought to herself.

"What's our move commander?" One of the 18th members asked.

Eliza opened her lids, flashing those emerald green eyes with firm conviction. Everyone wore the same stare of determination. All eyes on her, awaiting her decision. Her judgment.

"First and foremost, we'll stop that robbery. The Tampa Metropolitan Bank is the largest and busiest bank in the area, right? We don't know when they'll show, so Brian and I will be there incognito as soon as it opens. I want the rest of the captains and no less than ten others to show up and station themselves on the rooftop three hours before the bank opens. On my mark, I'll want you all to drop in and start taking em all out. Robby. I'll need you to disable any surveillance feed in the bank that catches our faces." She ordered.

Eliza walked around to the front of her desk and whipped up her sword. "This will be our first mission in broad daylight. I'll admit, I got a bit carried away at the casino and killed unnecessarily."

"Yeah, you ain't just whistling Dixie..." Slater added with a chuckle.

"Tomorrow, they're will be no casualties, not even for the robbers. With the attack happening in broad daylight we need the hard working citizens of Tampa to see us for what we are. Not another gang trying to make our marks, but a militia stepping up to corruption." She told them.

"And the superintendent?" Brian asked.

"One at a time, Mr. Wells. One at a time. Besides. The more and more I think about it, the more and more I'm beginning to believe this so called devil had some part to play in my father's demise. Until I get to the bottom of it, I don't want him touched." She warned with a creepy smile.

...

The Tampa Metropolitan Bank was located directly in heart of the business district of Northwest Tampa, just two miles away from the international airport. The next morning, as ordered, Sinus, Priest Edwin, Slater and seven other 18th Members positioned themselves on the rooftop of the massive three-story gothic stone building at a little past four in the morning. The skies were clear, there was no wind, but the temperatures were at a bone-chilling twenty-eight degrees. The men were all bundled up in thick electronically heated coats, already wearing their facemasks.

Eliza and Brian showed later, fifteen minutes after the bank opened at eight. They were posing as father and daughter with Brian using a fake name to apply for Eliza's car loan. The pair had made themselves comfortable in the large tennis court-size waiting area that was already packed with about two hundred other clients and customers, all surrounded by twenty-eight teller windows in an L-shape design.

Weapons weren't allowed in the bank and Eliza couldn't wear one of her hooded overcoats without witnesses giving a possible description to an officer. So instead, Eliza was wearing a durable faded-red flannel jacket, blue jeans and brown farming boots. She didn't have her sword or any weapon on her, but carried a plastic green facemask folded in her back pocket. Her makeup was exaggeratingly heavy and her blond hair was crimped with stripes of caramel coloring. The only accessory she had on was an assortment of six of her personal bracelets around her wrists.

As expected, it was loud and busy. The cheerful upbeat service androids that greeted patrons who entered the bank only added to the ambiance of chatter. An orange morning glow poured through the rows of symmetrical windows and commercial skylights to bounce off the crème colored walls illuminating the room. Brian was taking his time; slowly filling out the paper work he was handed. Eliza maintained the act of a young woman who was agitated by a migraine, slouching in her chair with her legs pulled in, covering her forehead with a jacket sleeve to block the sunlight. With her Furyx induced hearing she focused in and out of dozens of private conversations, hoping that one of the robbers was already present.

With a squinting gaze, her attention was elevated to the veranda of the second floor. An accountant was receiving a sound scolding by his rich client for mishandling a transaction for a boat loan that got repossessed. Eliza could also hear that Slater was still giving Sinus a hard time about his origins on the rooftop. It bothered her but she understood Slater's frustrations. With Eliza being the commander, even she thought it was foolish not to thoroughly check out the background of each and every member. She was aware that the men were placing an absurd amount of trust in her as well. Whatever the case was…Slater's attitude was getting out of hand. Sinus was a fellow captain. The only one he needed to answer to was her. Not Slater.

After two hours of waiting, the team's diligence paid off. Brian was too busy reading a book that was hidden within the folder of financial paper work. Without raising alarm, Eliza kept her head calmly propped up by her armrest and simply shifted her gaze to give Brian a signal. The fact that he wasn't paying attention caused her to roll her eyes.

The undercover Det. Parcell had just entered the bank and was approaching. He kept putting his hands in his pockets after using them, from opening the door to guiding an android out of his way. Even after he used a touchscreen to give him the current customer wait time, he kept putting his hands in his pocket. Eliza assumed he was nervous, no doubt concentrating on maintaining his cover as a genuine mobster. Eliza noted the three larger males in blue collar clothing that Parcell kept glancing at. They were already sitting in the waiting area not far from Eliza's position.

Parcell made his way to an island counter that was on the outskirts of the waiting area while Eliza watched by twirling a finger through her hair. There was another touch screen embedded in the countertop asking for Parcell's financial information. After inputting it, Parcell would receive a printed number with an assigned teller station that would call for him. But Parcell didn't fill it out. He tried to at least type his fake name, but his fingertips were too moist, his hands too sweaty.

Eliza gently grazed her elbow into Brian's ribcage. "He's here. Don't look. Be ready." Eliza told him.

Brian was a twenty plus year agent who didn't need to be told not to look around. But without taking umbrage, he simply nodded before putting up his book and going back to diligently filling out paperwork. Eliza stood up and casually approached the counter. The three burly accomplices in waiting watched her. All the makeup and bad fashion choices in the world couldn't keep a testosterone driven poon hound from ignoring that walk, those hips, that figure. Oddly enough, they seemed to lose interest when they saw her intentionally brush up against the side of Parcell.

The undercover cop turned startled. Eliza smiled at him with a nod. "Sorry bout that." Keeping calm with a friendly disposition, Eliza reached for another touch screen and started filling out blanks.

"Cold as heck out there, isn't it?" Eliza asked casually.

Parcell stared at her with a bewildered gawk. He then looked past her to see a muscular gray-haired man approaching to get in line for a teller. The man, a veteran enforcer named Teal, shot Parcell a stern glare to get ready before he himself faced a female teller.

"Listen." Parcell whispered softly. "Don't look at me. Just keep doing what you're doing."

Eliza held back a smirk as she followed his instructions. With his eyes intensely focused on his own touch screen, Parcell continued. "Now, I want you to count to five. After that, get you and your father and calmly walk out the front doors. Don't stop. Just go. Now."

Suddenly, there was a blunt metallic thud followed by two thunderous shotgun blasts. Horrific screams echoed out as Eliza's eyes whipped toward the front entrance. Two men wearing skull-patterned ski masks had just entered and knocked out the front security guards and destroyed the greeting service androids. Eliza turned back to Parcell. He too was now wearing a black skull patterned mask.

"Get down!" Parcell growled before shoving Eliza down under the island counter. He then climbed to stand on top of the countertop and pulled out a handgun.

Mobster underboss Simon Casker was the only masked man not running for the tellers. He was a gigantic man, well above 6'6. He had a thick husky British accent and was wearing a long brown trench coat. Simon casually strolled through the aisle around the waiting area with a shotgun slung by a strap around his shoulder.

"Alright everyone! Y'all know what the bloody hell this is! Get down and stay on the ground. Anybody move and we'll blast the tomatoes out your skulls. It's as simple as that." Simon said in a casual laid-back tone.

The 216 terrified men, women and children in the waiting area were already scurried about, lying face down, hiding behind columns and covering their heads to keep from seeing the faces of their captors. Eight armed men in skull masks had to sprint up the stairs to subdue and gain control of the bankers and clients on the second floor tier. Although three silent alarms were already triggered before the robbers could pin them down.

"Don't be afraid!" Parcell shouted as he stood above Eliza. "We're here for the same reasons you are. We just want some money."

Upon hearing Parcell's words, Simon chuckled with a shake of the head.

Eliza's eyes scanned the room from her squatting position under the island counter. There were sixteen robbers in all. Only two carried shotguns while the others carried electrical stunning nightsticks and projectiles. Then her gaze shifted up to the skylight. She could see Slater peaking in. She glared at him and shook her head no. Slater caught the petrifying warning and quickly got out of sight. She then turned her attention to Brian. The father of two was busy comforting a middle-aged mother and her three daughters who all still had to be in elementary school. Eliza could hear Brian telling the girls that everything was going to be all right. It was endearing sight, and as much as she found Brian's skills vital for the mission, she didn't want to put him or the family in harm's way.

It was time to move. Eliza nodded to herself as she reached into her pocket and pulled out the cheap plastic green facemask. Simon was approaching. He took a shotgun from one robber and tossed it up to Parcell who was still standing on top of the counter just above Eliza. Parcell caught the gun with one hand before tucking his own handgun back into the front of the pants.

"You know what to do, don't you Kravitz." Simon reminded. Parcell nodded.

"Well then. Take your pick. And be quick about it, eh. I don't care who. Heh. Surprise me." Simon said.

"Surprise!" Eliza shouted with cheerful glee.

Simon turned around just as Eliza sprung up from the counter behind him. Before he could even voice an insult, she whipped out a lightning fast jab to his throat that staggered him. As Simon put his hands around his neck and gurgling to breath, Eliza followed through by clamping the back of his neck and shoved him face first into the round edge of the granite counter with a cringing cracking thud that echoed off the walls. Simon's huge unconscious body dropped instantly with blood gushing from his broken nose and front teeth that were turned inward. Parcel watched frozen in place as Eliza clawed off her red flannel jacket to reveal a dark-green military tank top.

"That's it! Let's move." Slater shouted.

August the 18th came crashing through the ceiling skylight windows by rope and grappling hooks. With a shower of glass falling all around him, Parcell stood there shaking nervously with the shotgun in his hand. Before he knew it, Eliza performed a swift roundhouse kick across the countertop to sweep the back of his calves clean into the air. As he fell back, Parcell threw up the gun before landing hard on the countertop and rolling to the floor. Eliza caught the gun in midair and aimed the muzzle at his face with one hand. Parcell gladly surrendered without resistance.

"Round them up! Hurry!" Eliza shouted.

Slater was the most active in the offense against the bank robbers, shooting rubber bullets at their necks and chest as if he were running an academy obstacle course. The gang's cattle prods were no match against the combine efforts of a pole swinging Priest Edwin and the swirling broadsword of Sinus. Brian and three other 18th soldiers kept the patrons safe by herding them to the shouldering walls of the bank's massive waiting area. Eliza diligently stood in place with the shotgun fixated on Parcell. She watched her men and commanded orders from her post, reminding them not to kill anyone with the reason that if she could restrain herself, so could they.

As his fellow robbers were being thrown around and chased like they were running from bullies on a playground, Parcell stared up at Eliza with his back on the floor. The way she pointed her fingers and barked orders at the larger grown adults…and the way they heeded her command as if she were some kind of Pharaoh that they worshipped…It was amazing. It was unbelievable. The men kept calling her commander…commander.

In less than two minutes, August the 18ᵗʰ had rounded up the sixteen robbers, unmasked them and tied them up by the front entrance. Parcell was the only robber who was tied up yet remained fully conscious. It moved him to see the diverse group of pedestrians applauding August the 18ᵗʰ with heartfelt gratitude. Even the bruised security guards stood by, clapping their hands with a proud nod. They did nothing to stop Eliza as she led her masked 18ᵗʰ soldiers casually toward the front entrance.

As a restrained Parcell sat watching the group follow Eliza out the front doors, he noticed that she turned to throw a subtle wink his way. The gesture sent a spark of electricity down his spine to erect goose bumps on his forearms. A sense of valor was renewed. August the 18ᵗʰ didn't steal a cent. Nobody died. The police arrived by transport chopper just half a minute later and took the bad guys away. The goal was accomplished. But the mission was far from complete.

Later on that day, Eliza performed her first solo mission. It wasn't one of violence but more so of reconnaissance. Foiling the bank robbery massacre was only step one of her mission. There was still the matter of the untouchable Blue-Eyed Devil. Simply planting a bug on him wasn't good enough. She needed to find out first hand just how deep he was in with the Rosenbergs.

At just past seven that night, Superintendent Miguel Lobos was enjoying dinner with the wives and husbands of seven neighboring district police captains at the five-star Italian restaurant of the Hotel McBarron skyscraper in downtown Tampa. Wearing her dark Army green hooded overcoat, Eliza weathered the frigid cold. She was hanging upside down from one of the foot long stone sphinx gargoyles that protruded from the gothic cornice above every arched window of the hotel. The dining room floor was packed with the rich families, special occasions and once in the lifetime experiences. Everyone wore stylish tuxedos, dinner suits or designer's dresses. In one corner of the room, there was even a live string band playing contemporary arrangements of classical music. With the numbness setting in through her fingertips, Eliza was beginning to prefer burning the whole place down to be done with it.

Of course the topic of conversation between Lobos and company was the sensationalism of August the 18th that was steadily gaining momentum on media outlets all over the country. No one had any information on them other than the fact that a young woman with blond hair and green eyes led them. The group still hasn't been given a name, so they deliberated about what to call them. They openly discussed the idea of paying the press to paint them out to look like criminals. They even pondered over how the group was able to conceal their escapes from the hundreds of CCTV monitors and satellite communications. The potential threat this sudden vigilante group imposed was unnerving to the dinner guest, to say the least.

Eliza squinted her eyes as she watched Lobos. While the subordinate police captains all seemed bent out of shape and stressed out, Lobos was extremely calm and laid back, sniffing his cigar and throwing subtle suggestive glances at the young wife of one of his captains. Just as two waiters approached to serve the main entrees for the party, Lobos excused himself. A minute after Lobos' departure, the young wife excused herself as well.

Eliza was hanging thirty-eight feet above the pedestrians walking sidewalk below. The violet backdrop of dusk concealed Eliza's appearance even though a golden glow of chandelier light from the hotel's interior washed over her. Even so, as she began to scale the side of the cornice, she moved slowly, gracefully as to not draw attention with any jarring movements. Her training along the terrain of Mt. Bukhansan was paid off well. The ridges of the building's gothic architecture made it relatively easy for her to maintain a good grip. It didn't take her long to maneuver like a spider to another façade of the building. She couldn't visually see Lobos or the wife, so she followed the strong scent of her perfume.

The wife, Gail Cummings, was a brunette in her mid-thirties. This former professional tennis player wore a white silk dress that was almost thin enough to be considered a negligee. With her two carat diamond earrings sparkling in the light, this stunning woman induced envy from almost every female who threw a passing glance her way. Her high heels echoed as they clicked on the beige low gloss vinyl tile flooring of the third floor walkway. This walkway was part of a beautiful spiral rotunda that overlooked other floors and a massive golden globe chandelier that hung in the center of the atrium.

The suave Lobos stood casually waiting with the proper posture of a gentleman near the walkway railing. He was wearing his usual sophisticated smile that hid well the fact that he couldn't wait to tear that dress off of her. To two met. They shared a subtle kiss. Then Lobos took her by the arm and escorted her to an elevator. Once on board the elevator, as expected, the two began to ravish each other as if they only had ten more minutes to live.

The elevator lift ascended to the tenth floor with a smooth ascension. Upon hearing the chime, Lobos restrained himself to pull Mrs. Cummings away. She couldn't stop smiling. The way he pulled himself together to be prepared for anything and or anyone made her want him even more. As she continued to giggle, leaning into his ear and tugging on his arm, Lobos released a smile that could no longer be contained. That smile, however, transitioned to that of grave apprehension as soon as the doors split.

There stood Cassandra Pierce, dressed modestly in a black dress and knee high boots under a lush gray fur coat. Two large Black Creek soldiers in black tuxedos and sunglasses flanked her sides, silently standing with their hands clasps in front. Lobos wasn't alarmed but more so caught off guard. Mrs. Cummings, however, had no idea what was going on. At best, she thought Cassandra was one of Lobos' numerous mistresses.

Cassie attempted to ease the tension with a gentle smile. "Don't be alarmed Mrs. Cummings. This is official police business. Normally we'd wait to meet with the Superintendent in the capacity of normal business hours, but I'm afraid we need his help immediately. It is most urgent, I assure you."

The oblivious Mrs. Cummings bought Cassie's explanation. "I see. Then I'll leave him to you."

Cassie simply nodded in gratitude.

Mrs. Cummings then turned to anxious Lobos and kissed him on his cheek, close to his right ear. "Don't keep me waiting." She whispered.

Lobos put on a smile to shoo Mrs. Cummings off the elevator. He tried to follow behind her but one of Cassie's flanking soldiers shouldered his way in to block his path. The soldier palmed Lobos' chest back on to the elevator. Cassie and the second Black Creek soldier followed them in before she pressed the button to head up for the roof.

On the ride up, Lobos couldn't stop staring at Cassie's perfectly formed ass. Even with her grey fur coat on, it still managed to draw attention. Her well-toned calves showed the mark of someone who never missed a scheduled jog. Cassie slowly looked over her shoulder and caught him scanning. Lobos made no attempt to hide his infatuation, simply smiling that charming smile that's brought a dime a dozen to one of his private suites. Cassie batted her long eyelashes and faced forward with a glimpse of a smirk that Lobos was only able to see barely.

"That's unfortunate. Mrs. Cummings seems keen on you. She fully entertains the thought of running away with you. I know how that feels. It hurts. Truly unfortunate." Cassie said.

Lobos chuckled. "How very thoughtful of you."

"You take too many chances, Miguel. Unnecessary chances. One day it will come back to haunt you."

Lobos chuckled again. "Considerate and thoughtful. There's two attributes one wouldn't normally associate with the house of Pierce."

A Black Creek soldier leaned closer to Lobos. "Sir, please show some respect." The soldier politely asked almost in a whisper.

"Hmph…" Lobos uttered under his breath, still wearing a cocky grin.

The elevator doors opened up to the freezing rooftop eighteen stories up. You could see a panorama view of several other skyscrapers, including the Pierce Corporation towering around it. The wide open space was fully illuminated by florescent floor lights and spotlights that surrounded the helipad. Nine female Black Creek soldiers were already stationed on the roof awaiting Cassandra's arrival. The soldiers had already swept the place for bugs and set up signal disrupters on the camera. Despite their preparation however, no one noticed that Eliza had climbed high up in the darkness above them. Keeping perfectly still, she was now handing upside down with her legs hooked on the bars of the radio tower. An effective vantage point.

Cassandra was the first to step off the elevator. With the whistling wind and cold air, she was prompted to tighten up the coat around her shoulders. "Noah wants to meet with you. Tomorrow." She told Lobos.

Lobos laughed as he finally stepped off the elevator lift. "Don't insult me, eh Cassandra. If the Rosenbergs want to meet. I only meet with the boss."

"Miguel! Today has been extremely frustrating. Right now, we have sixteen of Noah's men lounging around in your cells. The House of Rosetti wants someone buried because they were kept out of the loop about the bank robbery in their backyard. You understand? They're out close to a million for failing to provide protection to a financial institution that has consistently paid their Bertie on time for close to a decade. Noah's reputation is on the line here. We can't have a top tier manager become an object of ridicule. Understand? And Bosco…Bosco suspects that out of the sixteen men you have locked up, there's a rat amongst them. He wants to burn all of them just to, as he says, "stop the plague before it spreads." This is really really bad, Miguel! Bad business all around. Please understand." Cassie stressed.

Lobos put his hands in his pockets and squinted those crystal blue eyes. "What does any of that have to do with you? This is between us men. Why are you here?"

Cassie raised an eyebrow. She couldn't figure out why on earth he was debating with her. She ignored his sexist quip and continued. "With this vigilante group running amuck, we can't afford for any of the Rosenbergs to be implicated. Thus, we can't have him afford to meet you…."

"If I'm implicated? Is that what you were going to say? Huh?" Lobos questioned.

Cassie stepped to within kissing distance of him, catching him off guard. If Lobos was a Casanova, Cassandra Pierce was a Mata Hari. Her seductive gaze and intoxicating perfume completely subdued his ego and pride as a womanizer. In her shadow, Lobos was reduced to a novice.

"What's the problem, Miguel? Hmm? This isn't like you. So what if its sixteen men locked up or even twenty? You've always been able to find a way for us. What's the problem?"

Lobos massaged the bridge of his nose. He wasn't the type of man who liked to admit his concerns, but was aware that he was already treading on thin ice. "There's an inspector in the ranks. A few, actually. But the keystone is this pious, self-righteous, stubborn cabron named Gazi. He's the thorn in my side, you see. I can't make a move without him documenting it. I can't take a piss without his musketeers Di Mare and Walsh watching to see if my aim is straight."

Cassie eyes pondered as she nodded. "Gazi...I've heard the name before. Where have I...Ah yes. Ben Garrett's bastard."

"I don't follow." Lobos said.

Cassie stepped back with a smirk, catching her own mistake. It was just a slip of the tongue to reveal a detail that she promised to keep a secret. Even though it was a slip, she was confident Lobos didn't notice. He had enough on his plate to keep him from wondering about Benjamin Garrett's affairs.

"Look, Miguel. Noah just wants to meet with you. Make that happened. As far as Gazi goes...He's the man investigating the Monteiro hit, right? If memory serves, and memory is my strong suit, Gazi's legit. Not on anyone's payroll, but too important to get rid of."

"Exactly. Can uncork a wine bottle with his ass, that one." Lobos added.

"Then give Noah some personal affect that they can use to frame Gazi. Tarnish his reputation." Cassie suggested.

"What?" Lobos uttered.

"Miguel! Good god, what's happened to you?" Cassie snapped with disgust. "You mean to tell me you couldn't have figured out a way to deal with Gazi on your own? Look, take my suggestion or don't. Either way, I don't want to ever see you again. I've known you since I was a little girl. You used to be spectacular. A capable man who knew what he wanted and took action, delicate action to achieve it. Not every problem needs to be solved with a blade or bullet. That's what you used to say to my uncle. Don't tell me this is what your legacy has withered to. Riddled away by a blonde girl scout and her band of merry men."

With those gripping remarks, Cassandra Pierce closed her eyes with disappointment before strutting past him to head back toward the elevators. Even with their sunglasses on, Lobos could tell her male and female security guards were all casting judgmental glares his way.

Lobos grimaced with agitation. The muscle in his cheek twitched erratically. "When does he want to meet?" He barked.

Cassie looked over her shoulder with her long black hair blowing in the wind. Her stare only exacerbated Lobos' overwhelming chasm of shame and embarrassment. It was like he was an old horse who outlived his usefulness.

"Tomorrow night. Nine pm. There's a car auction at the Durham Expo Center. Make me proud again, Miguel." Cassie said as she twirled her finger to a nearby female Black Creek soldier.

The female squad captain then signaled for the other soldiers to line up in a double file to make their exit. Four female Black Creek soldiers positioned themselves on the elevator around her while the others made their way to exit through the access door to the stairwell.

Lobos took in the last sight of Cassandra's heart wrenching gaze as the elevator doors slowly closed. A lump swelled in his throat. For a moment, Lobos contemplated throwing himself over the roof's ledge. Then, his worst fears began to race through his cognitive. He knew Noah Rosenberg was a brute who favored unsavory street tactics more so than his older, more rational brother. If Noah was angry enough, he wouldn't think twice about killing a high-ranking official. And when Lobos' body would be found floating in Blade Lee's Riverview water grave several weeks later, not a damn thing would be done about it. In fact, his reputation would've probably been all shot to hell. They would air reports about his corruption days on end, for weeks. These were the thoughts coursing through the Deputy Superintendent's mind.

After deliberating for ten minutes, Lobos wiped the cold sweat off of his forehead and took out his cell phone to place a call. He spoke in Spanish. "Javier. Javier, listen to me…I might need your help, brother. I'm in trouble. If I don't play my cards right, I may be a dead man. If you don't hear from me the day after tomorrow, I need you to find me."

As Eliza continued to watch from above, she wanted to slap herself for not bringing some kind of recording device. The excitement and refreshing satisfaction made her smile uncontrollably. It was as if she had just stumbled onto a buried treasure chest…and there was a lot of gold.

Not only did she have firsthand proof of the superintendent's involvement, but she now got the broad strokes of how the syndicate operated. The delicacy of the relationships and how fragile the seemingly formidable empire really was. She also saw the face of someone who had to be extremely close to either Braden Pierce or the godfather himself. No doubt, identifying where Cassandra fit in the grand scheme of things was a whole nother ball game, but one thing was certain with Eliza's priorities. Anyone who posed a threat to Gazi had to die.

The next night, Lobos showed up at the Durham Civic Center in the Pinellas Park district at a quarter to nine. The grand car auction was already packed with collectors, investors and fans alike. Light entrancing techno music sounded from the speakers and everyone was dressed with flash and expense, like they were coming from a music video award show.

The showrooms were filled with not only the latest sports cars and luxury convertibles, but also fully restored classics from the early 2000s and 2100s. There were the latest drone models and hovercrafts that still needed to pass Imperial clearance inspections on display. Exotic import models and go-go dancers were warming up, spicing up the already hedonistic atmosphere. In such an environment, their handlers seemed powerless to stop certain individuals from taking advantage of these bikini-clad models. But the ladies didn't seem to mind. It all came part of the territory.

Deputy Superintendent Lobos was dressed in a dark tuxedo and blue tie that matched his eye color. With a belied calm and confident demeanor, he looked around at the exits in his vicinity. He had off-duty police officers in plain clothes covering the exits, all concealing electric Tasers and daggers under their sports coats. These police officers were all either in his debt or someone who believed his promises of ascension. Either way, their assignment was to protect the superintendent.

At nine o'clock on the dot, a tall thin man with glasses named Harry, bumped into Lobos. Harry was wearing a wild blue tropical shirt and skintight brown jeans. Aptly named, Harry was indeed hairy, from his braided chest hair to the perm in his beard and mustache. Lobos quickly turned to accost the man but Harry smiled with his hand up to stop him.

"The Hayslett Room. Now." Harry said, shouting over the music and chatter.

Keeping his cool, Lobos simply nodded and turned toward an exit. He gave a stern nod to an off-duty officer who locked eyes with him. Picking up on the signal, the cop spoke into his wrist microphone to rally the others. One by one, the undercover cops slowly made their way out of the main showroom and into the less crowded hallways.

The lean towering Harry caught sight of the now not so inconspicuous off duty officers but casually continued to lead Lobos through the guests to another showroom. In this large showroom, the only music you could hear was the booming bass from the techno that penetrated through the walls. The Hayslett Room mainly showcased an assortment of flashy speedboats and vintage schooners.

With a warm smile, Harry gestured to the conspicuous off-duty officers in the hallway to follow Lobos into the ballroom. It wasn't until Lobos beckoned them in with an uneasy wave that the officers entered en garde. Once all were in, Harry closed the two-leaf doors and locked it.

Noah Rosenberg was already there, sitting at an end-table whilst eating a bagel that was smothered in cream cheese. Eight of his most trusted enforcers accompanied him, all of Jewish or mixed Jewish descent. And they were all wearing some loose fitted designer shirt with a sword at their side and a tucked handgun with live 9mm rounds. Noah was a large forty-seven-year-old man with short black hair and thin eyebrows on a forehead that seemed to protrude into a canopy over his hollow gaze. He spoke in a British accent and always dressed in some dull-colored business suit with a colorful tie that never matched.

Noah chuckled at the sight of Lobos being entouraged by six nervous plain-clothes officers. "Well would you look at this, eh? Has to be the first time I've ever seen a fucking wetback pulling the leash eh?" Noah said in rich bass-heavy laughter.

Noah put down his bagel and stood up from his table, removing the smile from his face in an instant. Lobos stood in place, with his sweaty palmed tucked in his pockets. Faking the confidence, he even appeared unfazed when Noah approached and used the flaps of his tuxedo as a napkin. The two stared each other down without blinking like heavyweight contenders attending their weigh-in.

"Must make you proud to have Mexico become a world power. Then of course, if I just sat back and watched the previous war from the sidelines, I'd be wealthy too eh? Picking the pockets of wounded on the field. Fucking disgraceful. The whole lot of you."

Lobos forced a grin. "Are we here to do business or pursue ah…historical trivia?"

Noah nodded as he stepped back. "I like that. This one isn't like the rest of em. No offense taken, eh. Always wondered which race was more sensitive. The niggers or the wetbacks? What do you think, Harry?"

"Do I have to decide, boss? It's a bit early to be bashing me own head in." Harry said igniting laughter from the Rosenberg ranks.

With his patience wearing thin, Lobos reached into his pocket and pulled out a small box before shoving it towards Noah's chest. Noah caught the box before it could fall and scowled. "What's this then? You givin me a bloody wedding ring? I have girlfriend." Noah said.

"It's a doctored statement from Gazi's credit company." Lobos told him.

Noah opened the box. Inside was a small thumb drive for a computer. "Oh yeah… Baby Cassie told me about that Gazi, fellow. Heh. He really that dangerous? You think this will be enough?"

"It should. Shows him paying for several of Nebraska Avenue's finest hookers. Also shows the purchase of a knife in evidence for the murder of a young black girl from Town and Country. That should suffice." Lobos told him before turning to walk away.

"And where's my eight-hundred grand?" Noah asked.

Lobos slowly turned with a wide-eyed look of absurdity. "What eight-hundred grand?"

"Its fifty percent of what my boys would've picked up yesterday. They're in your custody. So until you get them out, I need that money for collateral, my taco eating chum." Noah said with his hands clasped in front of his waist.

Breathing hard and shaking with rage, Lobos was finally beginning to break from the act.

"Oye!" Harry called out.

On the other side of the room there was a man wearing a cap in a gray janitor's uniform mopping the floor. The janitor had gone unnoticed the entire time. His back was turned on the group so no one could see his face.

"You! Fuck off, then! You can mop up when we're done." Harry barked.

The janitor didn't respond. Not even with a nod.

Lobos pointed his finger at Noah's face and shouted. "Cassandra never told me about any money exchange!"

Noah found Lobos' lack of composure amusing. "Well Cassandra ain't the bloody pope, now is she?"

"I don't have $800,000!" Lobos stressed with an insane wide-eye gawk. "Where on god's green earth do you expect me to get that kind of money?"

"Hey, hey, hey! Calm your tits, eh. I don't want to be unreasonable, times are hard and all that. We could always keep you company while your chums here go fetch it." Noah suggested.

"No! I'm leaving here with my man, and you're not getting a flipping nickel. You hear me." Lobos shouted chin up before spitting in Noah's face.

Noah calmly wiped the spit off of his brow with his tie. "See what I mean, Harry? Disgusting animals, the whole lot of them." Noah drew a long broad sword from the sheath of his closest enforcer.

Everyone else followed suit, drawing their swords and pulling out handguns. Lobos was the only one without a weapon, but he wasn't afraid. He was out of his mind. Ready to die in the blaze of glory rather than continue being held over a barrel.

"You're a dead man, Miggie. Guess this is where your prestigious career is cut short." Noah told him while waving the tip of his sword in a swerving motion.

"No wait!" Someone shouted in a creepy whispery rasp.

Everyone turned and looked to the janitor who was now standing closer to the group. It was a freaky-eyed masked Priest Edwin. He was aiming a crossbow in each hand.

"Please. Allow me." He beseeched.

Priest Edwin fired. One arrow struck Noah in the center of his throat. The other arrow scraped the lobe of the superintendent's ear before lodging into Harry's left eye socket. Unleashing a loud bloodcurdling scream, Harry gripped the arrow and staggered back. With a sorrowful gaze, Noah dropped to the floor in a death rattle as blood rushed from the hole in his neck. Suddenly nineteen masked August the 18th soldiers sat up from their positions inside the boats. Each 18th soldier was holding a crossbow aimed at either a cop or one of Rosenberg's men. Completely surrounded, the opposition dropped their weapons and put their hands up in submission.

As if he wasn't already stressed to the max, Lobos' now red strained eyes elevated from Noah's departing soul up to Priest Edwin. A wave of unimaginable horror began to take him, completely ignoring the pain from his gashing ear.

"Who are you people? What do you hope to gain from doing this? Surely you've thought this through. This man…He was nothing compared to the demons he served. Who are you?" Lobos shouted.

"Gee whiz…So much talk about demons and devils. I hope you guys don't actually believe that shit." Said the voice of a clear-toned, vindictive young woman.

Priest Edwin sighed emphatically as he lowered his twin crossbows. Eliza had entered through the two-leaf doors fully dressed in her hooded green overcoat and facemask. After approaching to within slapping distance, she let her golden blond hair flow freely by removing her hood.

Lobos backed away from her in astonishment. "It's you isn't it? You're the one who killed Sofia Monteiro. Who are you?"

In a quick blur, Eliza lifted her left hand to jolt the butt of her sword handle into Lobos' throat. The superintendent dropped to his knees and struggled to breath as the throbbing pain in his neck spread. Eliza then turned to Priest Edwin.

"Get everyone tied up. We have two minutes. Gazi's friends are on their way." She said in a bold authoritative tone.

Priest Edwin nodded. "Everyone. Put your hands behind your head and get against the wall. Let's move!"

The cops and Rosenberg men alike all hurried at the sound of Priest's naturally frightening voice to do as he commanded. Lobos was still on his knees coughing as the varicose veins began to swell and bulge from his neck and forehead. Despite the intense pain engulfing him to the point of inhumane torture, he still felt the urge to warn.

"My love. Don't you know what will happen? You can't win. You're not the first to try and take on the syndicate. Hundreds have tried. Hundreds have died!" Lobos strained to tell her.

After a brief examination, Eliza lowered herself into a squat. Then she grabbed his neck with one hand and slowly began to lift herself into a stand. And when she was standing fully upright, she continued to raise her arm, lifting him clean off the ground. The off-duty cops who were getting tied up all gawked at the sight, prompting several 18th soldiers to turn and stand amazed. The sight of a 130-pound girl effortlessly lifting a 220-pound man as if he were nothing but a large stuffed teddy bear poked so many holes in physics. Even Priest Edwin was stunned by the sight, but managed to urge everyone to continue in their progress.

In her deceiving bass-heavy voice, Eliza warned. "Superintendent Miguel Lobos. Blue-Eyed Devil. I have no doubt that you'll take to the streets campaigning your innocence and that your involvement with the syndicate was completely coerced and against your will. But I know the truth. We know the truth! We are August the 18th! We have taken it upon ourselves to act as judge, jury and if need be, executioners. And I am their commander."

Then with a quick jolt of her biceps, she yanked Lobos in closer and tightened her grip. Her glaring green eyes tightened into a squint and for this, she made sure to have his undivided attention regardless of much pain he thought he was in.

"If I ever find out that you've plotted against Inspector Detective Gazi again, if I even find out that you've ever mentioned his name again. I'll kill you. You'll be signing your own death warrant." She growled.

Lobos saw the feral tone in her eyes. The green around her pupils. The dark pupils that seemed to enlarge like a big cat on the prowl. Her threat aside, those intense green eyes was what made Lobos begin the shudder into a mild seizure. With that, Eliza released Lobos as if he was a cloth tainted with disease. The superintendent fell hard on his side. Within seconds, Lobos began to drift into unconsciousness as the flow of blood struggled to rush back up to his brain.

...

Lobos woke up sixteen minutes later sitting with his back against the wall. A young female paramedic intern was applying an ice pack to his forehead. A CSI unit was already on the scene with Noah and Harry's dead bodies covered where they lay in the center of the showroom. Most of Lobos' and the Rosenberg men were already in handcuffs and brought outside for questioning.

Deputies struggled to get rid of the reporters who had squeezed their way into the civic center. Everyone was trying to get a shot or scoop of the renowned police superintendent. The scent of a scandal was strong, and the weeks' worth of headlines needed a histrionic photograph to accompany it. If that wasn't enough, Rosenberg affiliates wandered through the crowd of onlookers. The death of Noah was the green light for a myriad of routes toward chaos. Danger and civil unrest were on the horizon and everyone could sense it.

Whilst faking a daze to keep the intern from asking questions, Lobos raced to come up with possible explanations. It didn't take him long to think of one, but knew that the timing of his card was crucial. He saw Walsh and Di Mare standing near a speedboat with a technician. Both were watching a laptop that was propped up on the hood of the boat. Lobos gently pushed the intern aside and used the wall to get himself up to his feet.

"Sir, please. You need to take it easy." The intern implored.

"Don't worry about me, angel. I'm fine." Lobos said with a polite smile before aggressively pushing her away by her shoulders.

Cautiously, Lobos began to make his way across the showroom whilst pulling himself together and straightening out his tie. He could hear the reporters shouting his name. In response he simply smiled and waved at the reporters like a seasoned politician, keeping in stride as he hurried to Walsh and Di Mare.

"Inspectors. Ah, Di Mare. My old friend. Thank god you're here." Lobos told him.

Both inspectors bore a glare of anger and suppressed contempt. "Superintendent Lobos, how are you feeling?" Di Mare asked with obvious disdain.

"Much better thank you for asking. Listen, I need to talk with you in private. Right now." Lobos stressed.

"Sir. Do you mind telling us why we found you unconscious in the middle of a showroom with a handful of convicted killers and thieves?" Walsh asked him.

"Do you two do everything together?" Lobos joked about with a nervous smile.

Walsh and Di Mare were not amused. Di Mare pressed his lips together in a cringe as he shook his head. The reality of their superior being in league with the underworld explained a lot. It made sense. But it did nothing to alleviate the massive blow to Di Mare and Walsh's pride as law enforcement officers. They were made to look like fools for so many years. So many operations gone wrong. So many convictions overturned. So many cases of missing evidence, witnesses abducted from safe houses and dead undercover officers. It took every ounce of strength for Walsh to restrain the urge to beat Lobos into a bloody pulp.

80

"Ah... As I was saying. I came here because I heard a few of my subordinates had some nefarious dealings with the Rosenbergs. That is, the infamous Rosenberg Association. I came here to try and persuade them to stop this nonsense, off the record. So I wouldn't be officially throwing the book at anyone. You know how that is, eh Walsh. Sometimes, especially these days, it's easy to be persuaded by the wrong element. Sometimes all people need is a second chance. Eh Di Mare? Walsh?" Lobos explained before releasing an air of heat from under his collar.

"Funny thing is…maybe if you had woken up a minute before we got here so you could've planted that story with one of the deputies. Then maybe we would've believed that stank bucket of horse shit!" Walsh shouted.

Lobos shook his head no in an erratic fashion. "Inspectors. Please. It's the truth."

"Deputy Hargrove said you came here to frame Gazi." Di Mare told him.

"No. He's lying! It's not true, Di Mare. Please believe me." Lobos stressed before speaking in Spanish so only Di Mare could understand. "These men. They're just lying to cover their own asses. Please Di Mare. I would never do anything to hurt your friend, Gazi. I'm the one who brought you into my division. Remember?"

Di Mare reached over to turn the technician's laptop so Lobos could see it. "We found a thumb drive containing a fraudulent credit card statement under Gazi's name. It has your fingerprints all over it. The document was created on a computer that has the same IP address as the computer in your office. How'd that happen?" Di Mare asked him.

As the idea of his defeat gradually began to sink in…a rumble of a chuckle gradually began to expel. The laughter gradually grew from that of mild amusement to a hysterical uproar. He keeled over and had to wheeze to breathe. It was getting to the point that the arresting officer had a hard time hearing himself read Lobos his rights as the insane superintendent was slapped in cuffs.

The reporters had a field day as thousands of flashes went off, each one trying to get the best shot of a mad man. As the officer escorted Lobos away, Lobos suddenly shrugged himself free but only for a moment. Seems he had one last message to tell the inspectors and would deliver it no matter how ridiculous he seemed.

"The group, inspectors! The group of vigilantes! They're calling themselves August the 18th. August the 18th! Hahaha! You may not know who they are. But their commander knows who you are. Especially that self-righteous bastard, Gazi! You tell him! Tell him eh! They know who you are! They know everything! Judge, jury and executioner! Their commander! She's a jaguar! She'll eat you alive! A jaguar! Hahahaha! There's a jaguar on the loose!!!"

Di Mare and Walsh watched the pathetic sight not knowing if they could trust anything else their fallen hero had to say.

"You're next!" Lobos continued to shout in his bout of madness. "If they brought me down, it's only a matter of time before you come down too! All of you! If I go down, everyone I've ever dealt with is going down! Senators! Mayors! Governors! Even the Provisional Emperor himself. No one is safe! This is only the beginning! The syndicate will have no choice but to release hell. This is war, inspectors! This is war!"

Chapter 16 – Strike Three: The Port of St. Petersburg

The fallout from Superintendent Miguel Lobos arrest was catastrophic. Anyone who was somebody wanted him dead. Due to the magnitude of how far his explicit web of connections stretched amongst world leaders, the matter of his protection was handled by the Imperial Secret Service. Testimony from Lobos and several inspectors called for the investigation of not only political leaders within and across state borders, but also against high-ranking officials in foreign countries.

Waves of protest sparked across the city with people demanding for the resignation of the occupants of several public offices including Tampa Bay's very own Mayor Bayne. Instead they had to settle for the suspensions of twenty-eight crooked cops and internal affairs investigations against sixteen district police captains. Anyone in power who has ever been documented associating with Lobos was in jeopardy of falling from grace. You couldn't go into an establishment without seeing the prognosticators talk about the future of the legal system. Debates went on in all corners. Suddenly everyone was a political science major.

After Lobos arrest and at the beginning of his media circus of a court trial, gang related activity increased with more aggression. Rebellious youths raised their middle fingers to the cops and surveillance cameras as they committed blatant thefts in broad daylight, from jacking luxury cars in the middle of the street to holding up whole supermarkets in the middle of rush hour. Sword fights and stabbings between rival gangs erupted. Business deals between drug traffickers got so out of hand with one party betraying the others that DEA agents would often show up on a drug bust just to see half the members of each gang hanging on to the edge of life from a loss of blood.

But it didn't matter. No matter what popped up over the city. By time the police arrived, the criminals were either dead or needing medical attention. August the 18th carried out missions with impressive stealth and minimal collateral damage. On the drop of the dime, whether it was day or night, there would always be one captain available to lead a group into battle. Throughout the first four months of the militia's existence, 62 filed assaults were reported against a group calling themselves "August the 18th". However, other than the casino raid, no civilian was hurt and every hostage was set free with his or her life still intact.

Eliza and Robby managed to keep their grades up in their classes. Robby began to put his trust in Stephen and Austin for hacking and receiving building schematics and decrypting radio transmissions. Eliza already had no doubts about the capabilities of her captains. Slater and Brian were effective natural born leaders. She didn't need to post assignments or even attend meetings about raids or infiltrations. She was simply notified and approved or disapproved of the missions beforehand.

From Brian Wells' point of view, Eliza was a diligent student. He had experience in training up and coming intelligence officers. Even though the two bumped heads on a number of occasions regarding the direction of the militia, Eliza always kept an open mind and wasn't too prideful to admit when she was wrong. Eliza already had a father figure in Gazi, so she wasn't looking for another one. Despite this, Brian saw Eliza as baby sister. It didn't matter if they were alone or in front of half the men in the group, Brian jumped on her anytime Eliza's childish impulses got the better of her.

A classic example of this was when she wanted to kill a suspected pedophile named Ashton Duphy without any conclusive evidence. Eliza was actually right in her assumption of the Duphy raping and killing dozens of girls, but without proof, Brian found her judgment and inability to articulate her reasons insufficient. Thus, Duphy became just like the dozens of other captured criminals, tied up and dumped in front of the precinct with collection of evidence pinned by a knife into their shoulders.

Slater and Robby still went at each other constantly. Where Slater had brawn and masculine charisma, Robby was clever and never afraid to deflate Slater's ego if it grew too big. Slater still had to maintain his appearance as a police officer working in the armory. And he was already well known in the precinct. Truth be told, several of his cop buddies already suspected him to be a member of August the 18th. But none were brave enough to oust him. Even if they were brave enough to report him, why would they? Slater was a man's man. A team player. He had your back and was dependable no matter how tense or dangerous the situation. The first man in and the last man out.

Sinus still preserved his mysterious aura and kept his captain status despite his lack of social skills. Eliza instead used his diminutive stage presence to send him out on clandestine missions. She tutored Sinus herself on the first five missions to show him some tricks to use in the art of ninjitsu. On several nights, Eliza and Sinus would carefully trail the rooftops and maneuver through fire escapes to follow and document the movement of biker gangs and drug pushers. Eliza had her hearing to rely on, so Sinus had to rely on sound magnifying earpieces that usually gave him a splitting headache the morning after.

Priest Edwin also remained a captain. He suffered a stab wound to his abdomen in early November but continued to be extremely helpful. He enjoyed teaching combat to anyone willing to learn. And anyone who received his combat lessons was forced to listen to his endless philosophy on religious cults and how most of the religions were manufactured by the will of a manipulating preacher. Much to the dismay of several members, Priest Edwin never failed to intervene in their personal lives. Often showing up at their day jobs and confronting them on an immoral act or sin they've committed. Eliza would receive complaints of Priest's behavior, but she and Robby found it all too funny to do anything about it.

National news outlets originally declared the group to be domestic terrorist organization. But after the first month of success resulting in the arrest of four fugitive Aryan killers, the media had no choice but to raise the malicious tainting label from terrorists to a pseudo-vigilante group. But shortly after, with the Rosenberg association in a disgruntled state declaring vengeance on August the 18th, the newsrooms began receiving death threats.

Journalistic integrity…

An ambitious ideology prompting several abductions and kidnappings. But the reporters and journalists held strong. And they weren't the only ones. Teenagers and college students alike were raving about the group in an excited fervor. Websites were popping up all over the Internet praising August the 18th's endeavors. It got to a point where the government began shutting the websites down. The younger generation responded by creating an encrypted forum that needed a password for entry access. Young adults from all over the world couldn't resist but to make August the 18th a viral sensation.

Other than jarring CCTV footage and on-hand witnesses, August the 18th had managed to avoid any altercation or arrest from the police. But the rumors of their leader being a young blonde woman with green eyes and a sexy physique were so abundant that she became an icon. Graffiti art of a masked Eliza became a rising trend. The government couldn't stop the endless flood of fan fiction and exaggerating paintings of Eliza leading her troops into battle. Eliza hadn't even thought of a logo or catchphrase, but thanks to their anonymous fans, they had one.

The adopted emblem of August the 18th was an anime facial portrait of what the teenagers thought Eliza looked like with a covered hood and spiked facemask in the tint of light green. It would eventually go on to change to something more artistic throughout the years, but for the time being, the emblem stuck. The sentiment the forums used when talking about August the 18th was that they were the "angels of the halo". And since no one knew Eliza's name, on the painting and labeling the graffiti of her depictions, everyone began calling her the Jaguar based off of Superintendent Lobos' ranting. And henceforth, Eliza's men referred to her in the field as commander or simply "Jag".

By early December, August the 18th had almost everything they needed to fulfill the ambition of the collective group to become a legitimate private militia. From the plethora of banks and business owners they saved, Eliza wasn't too bashful to accept donations of gratitude into a private Cuban account set up by Robby. Not to mention the money they confiscated from the casino raid. They even accepted eleven new members, all ex-military badasses. They had the money. August the 18th had the capital. They had the man-power. Now all they needed was a popular public opinion. A public spokesperson would be tremendously beneficial.

While the good hard-working law enforcement officers of Tampa Bay were grateful and felt some degree of safety knowing that there was someone out there in the shadows working in their corner, they couldn't help but feel some sense of shame and helplessness. Inspector Detective Gazi was one of those hard working officers. It was getting tough for Gazi and the other inspectors to walk out of their offices and hold their heads high amongst their subordinates. And while Gazi was somewhat idealistic and progressive in his morals, he wasn't stupid or oblivious. The reports about August the 18th were too consistent. It didn't take him long to suspect the college student living under his roof might actually be the city's own prowling jaguar.

Many long days passed with Gazi sitting in his office late at night, watching reports of his ex-girlfriend Michelle Hausermann projecting her opinions on August the 18th and dishing out back-handed jabs at the incompetence of law enforcement. He'd watch the footage of scores of known mafia associates and drug dealers being escorted to the back of a bus, all handcuffed and battered and bruised beyond belief.

"There's no way she's capable of this…" Was what Gazi would think.

With Gazi's hectic schedule and Eliza being in college doing what he assumed young college girls did on their free time, it was rare that Gazi and Eliza engaged in a face-to-face conversation. Most chats happened over the phone where Eliza would step off to the side during a mission. She'd convince Gazi that she was either studying or going to some sorority party at a campus house. But in the middle of December one Friday morning, there came a moment where the planets aligned. By coincidence, Eliza and Gazi were eating breakfast at the dining room table at exactly the same time.

With winter around the corner, Eliza was dressed in an adorable white sweater and black designer jeans, while Gazi sat in his district issued heavy padded sweater over his shirt and tie. Soft white sunlight poured in through the windows casting a bright glow on the dining room. Both were eating the same meal that consisted of a bowl of oatmeal with fruit and toast. Both were reading the news on their own individual electronic tablets. The Rottweiler, Max, sat staring on the floor in between them. With its drooping ears and lowered head, he seemed to be bored not with the awkward, but almost annoying silence.

Gazi and Eliza were aware of their absence in each other's lives. Gazi was a trained detective. Eliza was a natural born investigator. While both pretended to read their tablets, they mentally played out the conversations they would've liked to have with each other.

Eliza knew there was no way she could bring up anything happening in the news without the risk of slipping some detail that wasn't released to the public. But in her life, there was nothing else going on. She didn't go to parties. Didn't go to clubs. If she wasn't studying in school, she was either participating in August the 18th activities or off in some secluded place reading the book itself.

Gazi knew that beneath Eliza's grown professional veneer lay the dormant feisty wolverine that was her nature. He was sure that at her age and with the amount of maturity she attained over the years, it would take a lot to push her over the edge. But to accuse her of anything illegal without proof or probable cause would be the strike to light the fuse. And being the older more experienced adult in their situation, Gazi acknowledged that he had to be the one to make the first move.

"How's school?" He asked, keeping his eyes on his tablet.

"It's fun. Can't wait for the break." Eliza answered with a nod, keeping her eyes on her tablet.

"Oh yeah? When is that? Is today you're last day?"

"Yes." Eliza reached for her coffee mug. "First semester done. Whup Whup." She said with an awkward lack of enthusiasm and a casual smile.

Gazi grinned. "I was thinking. Since today is your last day. Why not start your break with me. Just the two of us. We can go to one of those new cyber flicks the kids are into nowadays."

Eliza smiled apologetically. "Oh! I'm sorry, Gazi. If you asked me yesterday I would've gladly said yes. But I already made plans tonight."

Gazi stared at her with those thick eyebrows and that thick mustache. In his personal opinion, he knew females were reserved by nature when it comes to men. But Eliza wasn't like most females. That doubt was just eating at him. It all made sense, but he didn't want to believe it. He couldn't accept it. He had to pry further.

"What plans?" He happily asked whilst displaying an innocent smile.

Eliza's green eyes rolled in a smooth controlled motion up to him. Her thin brown eyebrows arched with curiosity as she uttered, "Hmm?"

"Oh. I mean. You said you made plans. I'm wondering what plans you have for the night. You have a boyfriend yet?"

Gazi clenched his teeth after asking. He knew he messed up. Rule number one when it comes to interrogation; don't provide an excuse for the suspect. His angst was getting the best of him.

Eliza chuckled at the thought. "Please. More men are the last things I need in my life." Eliza's smile swiftly faded when she realized what she just said. Leaning forward, she pulled her hair back with one hand and quickly took in a spoonful of oatmeal.

Gazi sunk his teeth in the clue that was tossed out, but did so with tact. "More men?"

"Hahaha! You know. Boys keep coming at me from left and right. I'm not sure I have the heart to reject anymore." Eliza said as she went back to her tablet and scrolled through as though something amazing had just caught her attention.

Gazi kept staring at her. After putting down his tablet, he folded his arms and leaned back in his chair. He could resist no further. "What do you think of this August the 18th group?"

Eliza's heart skipped a beat. But as she looked up and noticed his stark skeptic gaze, offense began to manifest. She knew that Gazi, at the very least, suspected her but didn't have the heart to come out and say it. But she also felt that he was a prick who was just now toying with her. She simply responded with nothing more than another spike of her eyebrows.

"I ask cause I know how much you loved Reginald Harvey's work. His book August the 18th. Didn't you talk about how it helped you overcome your thoughts of revenge and animosity?" Gazi asked.

"Yes." Eliza said as she dropped her spoon into the empty glass bowl that followed with a light chime. "What's that supposed to mean?"

"Well, I mean. If someone was using the works of someone I cherished to go out and kill and take the law in their own hands like some kind of goddamn Robin Hood... I don't know. I guess I'd probably be a bit teed off. But that's just me." Gazi said before petting the top of Max's head.

Eliza's gaze shifted down to Max as her mind focused to contain her facial reactions. She was being interrogated. Gazi played his cards well. But there was no way Eliza would fold under such weak-kneed attempts to force her hand. She simply put the tablet down on the table, and grabbed her bowl and coffee mug to stand up and head for the sink.

"Elizabeth, I'm wondering why you're having a problem sharing your thoughts on the subject." Gazi said.

Eliza turned to him with a playful smirk. "Can I think? Gosh, Gazi. You ask such a deep question. Since our discussions are next to non-existent these days, I'd like to give you an answer that should satisfy you for weeks...hell, months even." She said with a cheerful tone before turning her back to him and rolling her eyes as she ran water through her oatmeal bowl.

After wiping her hands on a dishtowel, she walked over and grabbed her brown book bag to open up on the dining table and make sure everything she needed was there. With an unwavering stare, Gazi watched for any twitches of her facial muscles or nervous fingertips.

"From what I heard about August the 18th, I think it's too soon to form to any kind of conclusion. I mean what? They knocked over a casino, owned by the mob. They stopped a bank robbery. They brought down arguably this city's most powerful corrupt police officers. And from what I've heard, that same official was planning to frame you of all people. So these August the 18th guys…I dunno. I guess they're cool beans in my book."

Gazi looked at the green-leaf designed sword that hung beside her lower back. "Do you take that with you wherever you go?"

Eliza sighed as she put a hand on her hip. "Gazi. I just told you all of that and that's all you have to say? What do you think about August the 18th? Tell me how you really feel."

"Well, Eliza. I'm an officer of the law. Do you even have to ask?" Gazi said as he stood up and looked her in the eye. "Doing whatever you want, disregarding the law and making your own brand of justice…That just isn't right."

Eliza's agitation began to boil over. As much as she loved Gazi, she couldn't help but find his antiquated sense of morality to be complete bullshit. "I'm saying though. If this group…"

"Look, stop calling them a group, Eliza! They're a gang. A bunch of organized criminals, no better than the Winters, the Barreiras or the goddamn Ho Sun Dynasty!" Gazi barked.

"Why are you yelling at me?" Eliza asked appalled.

Gazi paused briefly to calm down. "What I'm doing, what my men do. They go out there every day and fight, put their lives on the line to uphold the law. They don't hide behind masks. They don't cut up men and beat them half to death leaving them out in the streets. And they don't execute women in their own personal version of a coup de grace."

Eliza looked stunned as she wondered what he was talking about. Gazi approached closer with an arrogant bobbing head nod. "Oh yeah. Haven't you heard? In that raid where they, as you put it, knocked over a casino. We found a secret camera in the vice-president's office. The vice-president was a woman named Sofia Monteiro."

Gazi picked up a butter knife off the table and moved it closer to Eliza. With a threatening stare, Eliza watched in toleration as he slowly pointed the tip of the knife at her throat.

"Mrs. Monteiro was already wounded. But just like that, this Jaguar…with long blond hair and green eyes. She stuck a sword into her throat. And she had a daughter, Eliza. Her daughter's name is Alma. It was just by accident in which I had to suspend a deputy that she saw the video. Just like you, she saw the death of a parent from the hands of a murdering psychopath. Now, Alma is traumatized. She'll never be the same again. Do you understand?" Gazi told her.

Eliza snatched the knife out of Gazi's hand before he could even blink. "Nice reflexes. One can compare them to say…cat like reflexes." He remarked.

As the two stood in defiance of one another…it was Eliza who began to release her emotions first. He was completely out of line but lost in the moment. After releasing a sharp exhale, Eliza wiped a thin trail of tears from her cheek and finished packing her book bag with the tablet.

"You know what, Gazi. Years after I move out of this place and you have it all to yourself. You're going to feel alone. You're going to think to yourself that it was because of your commitment to the job. That it was your dedication that kept you from holding on to people in your life. But I want you to know something. And please believe me when I say this because I mean it from the bottom of my heart and I want you to change. It won't be because of your job. You're like an uncle to me. And you always will be."

Her words hit Gazi like a ton of bricks. A lump began to form in his throat as he took his proud hands out of his pockets and settled them on the back of a chair. He kept his head down as Eliza swung her book bag over her shoulder and grabbed her green overcoat from off the living room. Just as she opened the front door, she turned to see Gazi still standing there with his head down. In the pit of her heart, she honestly did want to apologize. She even wanted to tell him that it was December 17th…Her twentieth birthday. But she was afraid. In the back of her mind, she felt it was better for him to not feel comfortable around her. The more distance between them, the better.

In any case, Eliza needed to get her mind right. Based on the stolen Intel from one of Superintendent Lobos' hard drives, August the 18th was set to face their most challenging mission yet. And it was all going down later that night.

Brian set a meeting with the entire group to be held that Friday afternoon at 3:45pm. Attendance was mandatory and given extreme priority. Eliza was usually the one giving the briefings, but this time she allowed Brian to address the group at the podium. Eliza herself sat in a chair beside Robby off to the side. Everyone was still dressed in their street clothing, but had their green combat gear in duffle bags nearby. They were seated in rows of foldable chairs as they listened attentively.

"Alright everyone. As Jag said, I appreciate you guys coming out. But I need everyone to be clear on this. Tonight. Bodies are gonna rack up. Cutting to the chase, soon after Miguel Lobos was arrested, we had Slater sneak Robby into evidence and back everything up. We're talking phones, hard drives, computers, the whole spiel. Most of Miguel's contacts in the force were smart enough to remotely erase any and all devices used to contact him. But some were slow. We spent the last several weeks combing through e-mails, planners, and calendars and thankfully, we were able to come across something."

Brian pointed to a large monitor screen hanging from the wall. A projector set up on an opposite wall displayed a surveillance photo of a Mexican male in his mid-thirties with fair skin and small in stature. He was wearing a light-blue business suit with golden thin-framed glasses and a beige fedora. In the photo, the man was speaking to a massive stadium sized audience in an open parking lot that spilled out into the streets. Everyone seemed entranced by what this man had to say with some holding up their fist in jubilance and others applauding enthusiastically.

"This is Madison Mariana Rios. I'm sure many of you have heard of this man. Especially you, Eliza." Brian told them.

Eliza furrowed her eyebrows, as she shook her head no.

"Really? That's surprising, seeing as this man also claims to be an Indivisualist. He was actually one of Reginald Harvey's closest friends. The man who wrote August the 18th." Brian told them.

"Madison Marianas Rios is a peace activist from the United Nations of Central America. After World War IV of 2112 when Mexico defeated the United States they became a world power. In addition to unifying all of the Central American nations from Panama up, they took along with parts of Texas, Cali, Arizona and New Mexico to form the UNCA. But of course, that wasn't the end of it. When Emperor Tremaine Rose rallied our country to resurrect it as the American Empire, dozens of skirmishes ignited along our borders, specifically the battles during the Neo-Hispanic war of 2162. The UNCA was itching to gain more territory and the Rose Dynasty wasn't budging."

"Just like with every war, there are people for and against it. Poor Mr. Rios was born in the midst of the war. He lost his brothers, his father and the near 5,000 acres that used to belong to his family due to HAZMAT pollution. Needless to say, the man has a strong chip on his shoulder."

"Since graduating with his PhD in contemporary philosophy, Madison has declared himself an indivisualist and embarked on a campaign to push for the UNCA congress to adopt a bill of rights similar to the constitution that the American Empire still uses today. The UNCA is officially a constitutional republic, but everyone knows it still follows a primitive democratic order where majority rules. Doesn't matter if they have an electoral college or not, anyone with half a brain intoned to the current events can see that they're just as tarnished as our own government. Needless to say, there's a bounty on his head. "

"Basically, he's spreading the same ideals Reginald Harvey preached, but he's doing it for the United Nations of Central America?" Eliza asked.

"More or less." Brian confirmed.

Eliza stood up and folded her arms as she walked to get a better look at the face of Madison Rios. She openly revealed her thoughts out loud. "Reginald Harvey was assassinated twelve years ago. He was a great man. A peacemaker. For the longest time I've always wished there would be another one like him and now we found him. We can't let Madison share the same fate."

Everyone gave a general nod in agreement.

Priest Edwin stepped forward. "It's a wonder he's managed to survive this long. From what I recall from the Nevada invasion, the Mexican army had a faction of influential war hawks in congress. They managed to pass a take no prisoners clause that was enabled for years, prompting public uproar from an already intense political atmosphere. With freethinkers like Rios running amuck, you'd think someone would've off'd him by now."

Brian nodded at Priest. "Yes, well the main difference between Reginald Harvey and Madison Rios is that Rios came from an affluent family. He has a dependable network of colleagues and followers who would gladly lay down their lives to protect him. Or help him to escape. This is what he's doing in this case."

Brian held up a remote and pointed it to a projector. It then began to display a video presentation of the satellite imagery in and surrounding the Port of St. Petersburg along the bottommost tip of the Pinellas county peninsula that protruded into both the Gulf of Mexico and the Bay of Tampa. It was the largest seaport on the Gulf of Mexico and the second largest in the American Empire. The footage showed rows and rows of docked ships, freight and commercial, along with close to a million cargo containers stacked up and sections by plots that looked like cubes from an overhead view. There were port authority watchtowers stationed at each of the fifty-eight terminals. Each three story watchtower building was equipped with armed security personnel and access to surface to air projectiles should the need for such measures arise.

"According to one of Superintendent Lobos' e-mails we decrypted, Madison Marianas Rios is being smuggled into the country through this seaport. He is said to be in one of the hundreds of TEU cargo containers along with over two hundred Mexican immigrants. These immigrants are the wives and children of other political prisoners and activists who have sent their families away amidst imminent threats from terrorist cells all suspected to be working under orders from someone high up in the UNCA's Presidential Cabinet. The expected arrival time is said to be at 2am tonight." Brian informed them.

"Now. Here's the problem. One. The cargo ship with Madison and the immigrants will be one of three 400 foot cargo ships coming in. Each of them capable of carrying up to eight hundred containers. We don't know which one will have Madison. And we don't know which container Madison will be in. This puts us at a slight disadvantage. The enemy, on the other hand will have said knowledge." Brian told them.

"And who is the enemy?" Slater said, getting impatient as if that's all he really wanted to know the entire time.

Brian used the remote to click to a new slide from the projector. The slide showed a group photo of over sixty ab bearing Haitian natives assembled as if they were taking a high school class photo. They looked as one would expect from mercenary pirates for hire. Riddled with tattoos, athletic and proudly boasting their weapon of choice, welcoming any and all challengers.

"Cube 28's Awakening. Or simply known as C28. They're a paramilitary group based out of Haiti. These are the men who accepted a $500 thousand dollar contract to take out not only Mr. Rios, but the immigrants as well. Their benefactors remain a mystery, but we know they've furnished C28 with boats, supplies, and three expert capoeira spear fighters from Jamaica. These twin spear fighters are well-known mercenaries who have performed hits for cartels all up and down the west coast of South America. They're called the Inca Trinity. And it's said that they have the Furyx Gene…"

Everyone became uneasy. Silent f-bombs began to drop amongst the mild whispers. Brian turned to Eliza for her input. Suddenly, a look of baffled horror took hold as he noticed her unnerving expression. Most of the soldiers in the group who have served and experienced amphibious combat all let off the same tense grimace of concern and outright fear over the possible outcome. But Eliza…Eliza was staring at the photo of the Haitians with a wide-eyed grin of anticipation. Sinus and Priest also noticed and shot glances of amusement toward each other. In the pit of their stomach, they too could feel some sense of excitement for the battle that awaits them. The feeling was electrical.

Robby rose up from his seat and approached Eliza with his hands in his pockets. "Eliza?"

Eliza snapped out of her trance and looked around. She saw the looks of impending dread from some. She also caught some who had noticed her enamored expression and were now staring at her like she had three heads. Eliza stepped past Robby and approached the podium to address her men.

"I know some of you may be concerned. And you have every right to be. I've told you about the Furyx Gene. If your average handgun can't bring these guys down, then neither will your spears, swords, and Tasers. I simply ask that you make the safety of those seeking refuge into our country your top priority. Leave the spear chuckers to me." She said with an extremely arrogant smirk that, oddly enough, put to rest the apprehension of many.

With that, the briefing concluded and the group broke off into smaller sects as Brian remained the only member still skeptical towards the outcome of the mission. He knew Eliza had passion. He knew she had the skill. But the odds of one Furyx user against three, and at her age…success for August the 18th looked grim.

...

The Port of St. Petersburg

Midnight came but the massive commercial seaport was lit up bright as business had no intention of slowing down. Longshoremen were still taking inventory and moving crates. Seadogs were still unloading the oil barrels from freight ships at twelve of the ninety-two massive berthing terminals. The entire port covered nearly seven miles of the waterfront. The port was visible to incoming ships from over thirty miles out with the golden glow of the Halo passing by just a couple of miles further away.

The Imperial Coast Guard handled the security jointly with the Port Authority. With the Port of St. Petersburg serving as one of American Empires main import and export point for the new Hispanic powers, the security guards were granted permission to carry assault rifles. A few August the 18th members were close friends with some of the security guards on staff for the night. Relying on trust and years of friendship, Eliza granted them permission to warn the security detail of the impending battle and asked for most of the guards to be stationed with the other civilian dockworkers on the eastern end berths on the side of Bay of Tampa.

One Coast Guard official who was impressed with the 18th's works returned their warning with one of her own. She warned that if the battle took over three minutes, they would have no excuse for their commanding officers as to why they didn't interfere. They would have no other alternative but to go in and take down mercenaries and 18th members alike.

Thus, after the briefing, August the 18th had spent the rest of the afternoon and well into the night hours preparing for the mission, memorizing the layout, planning the entry and exit points. After going over the objectives, Brian and Slater both agreed that the probability of the battle lasting under three minutes was too unrealistic. They knew that they were going to have to deal with the National Guard and planned out measures to handle them with care.

The 18th were to be divided into three units. Brian would lead the third unit to station themselves spread out at the eastern most point of the western terminals. All of his 14 men were equipped with high-powered scoped rifles that shot beanbags. Their objective was to pick off as many tangos from C28 as they could, but mainly to subdue the National Guard and keep them from entering the fray when the three minutes were up.

Slater and Sinus would lead the second unit to drive a frontal attack against the main force of Haitians. They were to position themselves at the southernmost point of the western facilities. Equipped with six high-density inflatable boats, Slater and his thirty-five men were granted permission to embark over water and pursue the Haitians that would pass through the third unit. They would be the main blockade to stop the Haitians from embarking on any of the ships.

Eliza would lead Priest Edwin and the first unit to serve as the second wave and main defense for the cargo ships in protecting the immigrants. She and her fifteen men were equipped with three high-density inflatable boats to pursue on water and board the ships should they need to. During the 18th's planning, it was debated on whether or not they should wait and let the Haitians board the ships to lead them straight to Rios. But Eliza made it clear that she'd rather go on the offense than defend, so she chose to go with the first unit to effectively do both. All units were to have their eyes open and weapons tight.

Other than the group's hackers and two men who were still in traction from a previous engagement, every single August the 18th member participated in the mission. Robby needed Stephen and Austin's help to handle frequency jamming and planting fake digital images in sections of the vast network of security cameras that watched over all the collective facilities and transport terminals. Then there were the satellite RSS feeds that would need to be hacked into. The job would've been too much for even the Pierce's top hackers. But Robby, Stephen, and Austin were up for the job.

At a quarter past midnight, August the 18th drove spread out over different roads all winding south toward the seaport. At two miles out, the 18th members parked their hummers and pickup trucks in a safe shaded area before hopping out and jogging the rest of the way. The rendezvous point was an abandoned trailer on a hill that overlooked most of the western facilities of the harbor. With the weather being just below twenty degrees, everyone was dressed warm, wearing dark-green, almost black colored military grade wetsuits underneath their electronic coats. Even Eliza wore a skin-tight green wetsuit under a dark-green raincoat variation of her overcoat.

Eliza treaded softly, letting out no sounds as she led her men over the frosted grass towards the chain-link electrical perimeter fences. Everyone stayed low to the ground and moved liked smooth fast moving shadows of clouds. There was a high watchtower fifty yards from their position. Snipers were perched up top in the look out.

While the group usually carried only swords, electronic spears and nightsticks out on missions, going against Furyx users required them to carry holographic dot assist assault rifles. There wasn't a word said between them. All you could hear was the various clicks and straps being pulled. The group performed a final checklist of preparation before planting their duffel bags in trenches under the trailer. Eliza didn't carry a rifle or any sort of handgun. Ivy and her assortment of ninja accessories were all she needed.

As the main group stayed hidden in the shadows of the trees, a lone soldier and technician named Halford moved forward toward the electrical fence and attached four rubber disrupters the size of paperclips on the chain links. Meanwhile, Priest Edwin kept his eyes peeled on the watchtower, hoping the three snipers station there wouldn't pick up on any sounds. If they did, he would have no choice but to knock them out with bean bags shot from a high powered rifle.

The disrupters Halford put in place blocked the flow of electricity in a thirty-inch circumference by which they were placed. The technician then took out a small black-handled laser saw that was the size of a shaver. With a click of a switch, a half inch superheated laser omitted like a flame from a cigarette lighter. There was a light constant sizzle as it steamed the icy salt moisture in the air. It didn't take long for Halford to cut a thirty-inch gap in the fence one link at a time. With a quick tug on the fence, the technician ripped out a manhole in the fence. He then turned around and held up an "okay" signal toward the trees.

Eliza nodded as she tightened her facemask and made sure her long blond hair was held in place by a ponytail bun. With an entry point now granted, she made her move. Using Furyx speed and cat like agility, she dashed out in the clearing and dove cleanly through the small manhole in the fence in a matter of seconds. Her men watched in awe as Eliza sprinted fifty yards in the open lit undetected by the snipers until she reached the base of the watchtower. Without making a sound, Eliza jumped up sixteen feet to grab onto a ledge and continued to swing herself up the watchtower wall like it was her own personal jungle gym.

Upon reaching the top, Eliza hung from the open ledge just below the view of an active sniper who was standing guard. With her Furyx-induced hearing, she was able to located where each of the three snipers were on the platform. One was standing right in front of her. One was sitting with his feet propped up on a ledge, leaning back in the chair and smoking a cigar. And the last one was standing beside the seated sniper, talking about how there was no doubt in his mind that his wife was cheating on him.

With one hand, Eliza reached into one of her coat pockets and pulled out a tranquilizer dart. After taking in a deep breath of icy cold air, Eliza swung herself with the other arm and injected the needle into the sniper's chest, knocking him out instantly. Before the sniper could fall, Eliza held him up with the same left hand and cautiously pulled herself up and into the platform. With the unconscious sniper appearing to lazily slouch against a railing, the remaining two snipers didn't notice Eliza slithering up behind them. After listening to them brainstorm about how women were natural born whores, Eliza relished the moment in stabbing tranquilizers into both of their necks at the same time.

With the snipers down, Eliza peered out towards the next nearest watchtower. It was over five hundred yards out with its occupants just as casual and relaxed as the men she just took out. Eliza waved back toward her main group. Five 18th soldiers followed the procedure of adding disrupters to the electric fence and cutting out larger holes. And through the six gaping holes, the 18th men infiltrated through the fence with and marched almost with a synchronized gallop toward the watchtower. She jumped over the ledge to meet them at the bottom.

"Let's keep our channels open and our eyes peeled. We have a job to do tonight gentlemen. Let's make it happen."

With that, the force split up into their three assigned units and headed out to their positions. Then, for the next hour and a half they would simply wait.

The first unit positioned themselves around an isolated warehouse filled with aluminum filing cabinets and outdated paperwork. Most of the men stayed out of sight, hidden in the shadows of the shipping containers. Some were smoking cigarettes, but more casually chatting amongst themselves recanting days of army tours served. Their commander was sitting twenty feet above them on the horizontal steel beam of a bridge crane with her legs dangling over the edge. The ghostly Priest Edwin was standing by her side. The both of them stared out west, watching for any sign of light.

After thirty minutes of nothing but silence between the two, Priest Edwin turned left and looked down at the blonde jaguar. If there were fewer years between them, he would've taken advantage of their solitary time together. The young woman was leaning back with her weight propped up by her hands. Her long hair was tied to the back, but loose strands of gold flanked the sides of those green eyes. Her beautiful face displayed an expression that seemed to say she was at peace, not worried in the slightest about the daunting task they faced.

Eliza glanced over her shoulder and caught him staring. She knew him well enough, but it was one of the first times she was alone with him. And what she found strange was the fact that she caught him staring, yet he didn't look away. Priest just kept staring at her.

Eliza pulled her facemask down from around her neck so no one with an earpiece could hear her over their communications. "Edwin…is there something on your mind?"

Priest Edwin looked down between the wide steel beams. It was a dangerous drop to the pavement below. Then he looked back over to Eliza. Her thin hazel brown eyebrows were lowered, confused and slightly annoyed at the possibility that Edwin might have bad news. While stepping with caution to approach her, he pulled out his earpiece and took off his facemask completely.

"Jag….Is Elizabeth your real name?" Priest began.

Eliza smirked as she nodded and pulled out her ear piece. "Is Priest Edwin yours?"

Raising a single eyebrow briefly, Priest shook his head no and he went back to peering toward the dark horizon. Eliza glowered with annoyance again. "Edwin, tell me what's on your mind."

"Do you mind if I speak frankly with you?" Priest asked in his usually whispery raspy voice. Eliza nodded.

"…Who do you think you are?" The instant the question left his lips, Eliza turned away from him, disturbed by the condescending question she's heard over a hundred times.

"Don't get me wrong. For someone of your age…and gender. To have done so much. You've gathered a group of kindred spirits to work together for a worthy cause. It's to be commended." Priest said before squatting down beside her.

"But I have to ask. Who do you think you are? For months we've been busting up gangs, exposing immorality in the justice system, protecting witnesses…it's all well and fine. But we've gathered under your wing because of the syndicate. They're killers. But then…so are we. Are we not?"

Eliza's breath was visible as she released a heavy sigh. "What's your point?"

"You have no experience. You haven't served in the military. You've never worked in a public office. You're only nineteen. A college freshman. What makes you think you have what it takes to bring down the syndicate? Mind you, even if we do take out Isaac and Braden and whoever else. It's still a corporation. Someone else will rise up and take their place. Do you intend to have us fight like this forever?" Priest asked her.

It was a lot for Eliza to take in. Priest Edwin's eyes hardly blinked. He watched as Eliza's eyebrows moved up and down emotionally in serious thought. He was actually relieved to see it. He didn't push her for an answer. But simply rose back to a stand and joined her in looking out toward the horizon. It was slowly approaching 2 a.m.

"You're right." Eliza finally spoke up getting Priest Edwin's attention.

"I don't have any experience. I've never served in the military. I don't know the first thing about guerrilla tactics or strategic warfare. I don't know anything about corporate structure or even the exact textbook definition of what a corporation is. And you're right. We are a group of killers. All soldiers are. And I'll admit that killing is morally wrong. Even Reginald Harvey spoke out against it."

"Exactly!" Priest exclaimed, cutting her off. "I have to say while I've heard of Reginald Harvey, I confess that I haven't read August the 18th until two weeks ago. This book was supposed to have brought you comfort when you were spiraling down a hole of abhorrence, right? You call yourself an indivisualist, but Harvey preached that human life was more important than money, religion or any other ideals. I've served with mercenaries and contract killers alike. But in the near four months I've known you…I've seen you slit a man's throat, light a building of drug dealers on fire, and decapitate a mob capo with one swing. Your personality is unpredictable, impulsive and inconsistent. Other than your desire to kill Braden Pierce, your goals with August the 18th are bleak. I don't know how the others feel about you. But anyone with half a brain would feel like a pawn in the game you're playing."

"You said you read August the 18th right?" Eliza asked.

"That's right."

"Then maybe, you just don't know what an indivisualist is." Eliza told him.

"Enlighten me." Priest responded.

Eliza shot him a squinting glare. "August the 18th preached about honesty. Harvey preached that those who lie are cowards. Cowards use lies and deception to build walls to hide behind. I believe in that theory and I hate liars. Because I hate cowards. What I lack in experience, I more than make up for with my capacity to take action instead of sitting back to just bitch. And I don't mind that you compare me to a mercenary or contract killer. You talk about me being unpredictable. But isn't that your fault? I barely know who you are, Priest Edwin. But I know what you will and won't do. But just so there's no confusion, let me break it down for you. And if you don't like what you hear, feel free to back out at the first sign of daybreak."

Priest raised his hand. "Hey. No need to take offense…"

"No, screw that! You better shut the hell up and listen." Eliza told him in a calm, yet stern tone. Priest Edwin was completely dominated and taken aback by her naturally emanating authority. Several of the men beneath them overheard and were impressed as well.

"The only reason why I'm telling you this is because I actually care about what you think. Being an indivisualist is about taking control of your own life. Yes, I agree with a lot of what Reginald Harvey said, but part of being an indivisualist is being able to pick and choose what you want out of a theory or philosophy. No one on earth will always be 100% right about anything. That's what people from the old millennia didn't get. Being a conservative or a liberal shouldn't be about agreeing with everything the majority dictates. Or how being black or white wasn't about being a part of a stereotype to feel unified and socially accepted with their own race."

"Your life is yours. Do whatever you want with it, Priest Edwin. As far as August the 18th is concerned. We'll fight the syndicate and continue fighting for generations if that's what it takes. But before I go…before my soul leaves this world…I will have Isaac and Braden's head. That's my goal as the first generation commander of August the 18th."

Priest Edwin's eyes opened wide at the thought of her calling the group the first generation.

"I'm not nineteen, Edwin. I'm twenty. And I might not have the experience. But you do. So do Brian Wells and James Slater and Sinus and most of the men we have with us. You're not pawns. When I see my men, I see each one capable of standing on their own two feet should anything happen to me. I believe that part of being a commander is being able to trust and depend on those she leads. Can I trust you, Priest Edwin? Can I depend on you to help me reach my goals?"

Priest Edwin stood well above six feet tall. And while Eliza was only sitting down and looking up at him, he felt like he was a pioneer overlooking the vast frontier. Not even his superior officers in the army had the nerve or honesty to blatantly admit their selfish goals then stand there and demand his support. But she did. Without shouting, without spitting in his face, without yanking him against a wall, she just sat there and asked for his loyalty. A young woman. Only twenty.

"You can depend on me, Elizabeth. The first generation of August the 18th will accomplish their goals and set an example for future generations." Priest said with a smile before putting back on his facemask and earpiece.

Eliza threw him a smirk. "Damn straight."

Priest Edwin shook his head, slightly amused with her obnoxious sense of pride.

"Hey! That's a load of garbage!" Slater complained over the radio. Eliza and Priest could hear him through their earpieces. The two glanced at each other with a sigh.

"And the word for today kids is irascible." Robby replied. A slight wave of chuckles followed.

"Can it, geek!" Slater barked over the communications.

Slater, Sinus and the second unit had positioned themselves on the loading docks in between a massive yard of shipping containers. The thirty-five soldiers had divided themselves into groups of five with one inflatable boat each, all spread out between the containers, not far from the water railing and the sounds of waves crashing against the docks. Apparently, Eliza and Priest Edwin had just plugged in their earpieces amidst a debate that had been going on for a while.

"How can you say that, Wells?" Slater barked.

Brian and his fourteen men of the third were positioned along the top of a warehouse facility about 300 yards from where the nearest harbor men were still using dollies to remove fuel barrels from the freight ships. Brian and his men were just out of view of the flood lights. While Brian was content with their conversation and satisfied with his oratory, his men were all wearing disgruntled looks. There were only so many Slater opinions a man could take.

Brian sighed before speaking into his facemask. "Slater. Christianity's been around for over 2,200 years. You say logic and religion don't mix, but logically speaking it just goes to show that there's a higher power behind it. Christ! Where's priest when you need him?"

Priest chuckled. "What's going on?"

"Whoa? Look who finally decided to join the fucking conversation." Slater barked.

"And that voice, man! Damn!" Another member barked out of agitated terror.

"Where were you? Is Jag with you?" Robby asked.

"Yes. She's next to me." Priest confirmed.

"I already told you that, Robby." A member from Eliza's unit reminded him. "You need to trust somebody, boy."

"Alright, religion aside, we're talking about this prick, Madison Rios." Slater began, already annoying Eliza.

"I mean. For starters he's coming from one of the leading world powers. Sure Brian gave us this whole spiel about how he's self-righteously calling himself an indivisualist, but anyone who's followed his speeches knows he's a devout Catholic. And this so called republic he's fighting for is really a hidden agenda for spreading an isolationist sentiment to get away from Imperial America."

"Dude! Where are your sources? Where are you getting this?" Robby mocked.

"What the hell do you know you little door mat. Stay in school and you might find out." Slater barked.

"Am I missing something here? Why are you so bent out of shape over this, Slater? And why just now?" Eliza questioned. "You had all goddamn day to vent your frustrations."

"I just can't stand hypocrites." Slater answered.

"No. What you are, is a force-fed WASP still living in your great-great grandfather's memoir of America. It's called diversity you suppressed supremacist. Deal with it." Brian answered.

"Now that you mention it, Wells. I think Sinus is the only non-white member of our crew. I wonder…" Slater mentioned sarcastically.

"Well…after hearing that. I don't particularly care to hear your opinions on religion." Priest Edwin said which brought about a general round of laughter.

Suddenly, Eliza's head shot up with alert. "Wait! What is that?"

Priest Edwin and most of the soldiers in their unit one turned looked to Eliza. Her eyes were staring off toward the horizon. She dropped down off of the beam and landed with a metal bending bang on the roof of a crane-controller's cockpit four feet beneath her. She squinted her eyes. But even with her Furyx, she couldn't see anything approaching. But she heard something.

"What the hell is that?" Eliza said aloud, mostly to herself.

"What are you hearing out there, Jag?" An 18th member asked.

Eliza knew she wasn't going crazy. Something was happening and it was happening now. "Damn. Robby!" Eliza called.

"Yeah Jag, what is it?" Robby asked.

"Are you getting anything on the satellite?" Eliza asked.

Back at headquarters, Robby, Austin and Stephen all wore puzzled looks as they sat in front of their computer stations. Robby had his hands raised in confusion. His computer screen showed the 18th' unit positions scattered throughout the western part of the sea port. Nothing seemed out of the ordinary.

"I'm lookin Eliza. And I see nothin other than you guys. Hang on, let me reboot the program."

Eliza finally caught sight several unidentified targets and lifted her hand to point. "I see them. The enemy is coming from the south. But still...I hear something larger coming from the gulf in the west." She said.

Robby typed a password into the program to refresh their green night-vision satellite feed of the seaport. "What the hell...Austin, refresh your screen."

Austin had his arms folded but quickly released them to type on his keyboard to refresh. His eyebrows quickly furrowed. "Oh crap! Someone else is hacking the same satellite feed. We need to get on this." Austin told them.

"Hang on. What? Somebody talk to me!" Slater barked.

Apprehension kicked in as Robby lifted his trucker hat briefly to scratch his head. "Look. You guys need to have your eyes opened. The satellite feeds are compromised. Don't trust what you see on the GPSs. Someone else has hack into the feed. We have to block em out, and fast. But the point is someone knows you're there, and it's going down now because our screen refreshes automatically every five minutes."

Back at the seaport, Slater stood up in fury. "You gotta be kidding me!" Slater shouted.

Suddenly automatic gunfire rang out. A spray of bullets clanged onto the metal containers just above Slater and several 18th soldiers narrowly missing the neck of one. "Shit. They're here! They're comin up from the south!" Slater shouted.

Brian and unit three could see that the dockworkers heard the gun shots. Amongst their panic and commotion, one of the workers set off an alarm that turned on a long row of stadium lights. These powerful beams of white light illuminated up to five hundred yards of the water around the entire port.

"Alright August the 18th, we got three minutes before the coast guard rolls through." Brian warned.

As Priest Edwin held up binoculars to look south, Eliza conveyed what she was seeing. "There are ten vessels. Small vessels. About forty plus tangos 800 yards out and approaching fast. Heading west."

"All right then! Let's boogie!" Slater ordered with zeal. He, Sinus and the second unit hustled to carry their inflated boats into the water. One by one the six boats raced off over the choppy seas towards the midst of C28's forces.

Eliza's men in the first unit were also in the process of carrying their inflated boats to the water. Priest Edwin ran toward the end of the steel beam he was on and slid down the side to reach the ground. Eliza was still standing fifteen feet on the controller cockpit with her eyes glued toward the west. Her heart started to pound.

"Oh my gosh. I see it. I see them!" She shouted.

Everyone in the first unit look out toward the west. They could only see the small shaded dots of something protruding over the horizon. Three massive cargo ships, all with flat decks only half full of containers, were speeding toward their location a half a mile out and closing. They were moving side by side. All of the lights were off on the ships and Eliza couldn't sense any visible sign of life. No sailors. No captains. No lookouts. They just looked like three mechanical ghost ships that were operating by themselves as they cruised over the chopping water.

As expected, the men of the C28 Haitian paramilitary group were all black natives dressed in thick faux fur jackets that were painted in splashes of neon green and orange, inspired from a popular hip hop music video. The second unit was already engaging them with Slater leading his men into a nautical gunfight.

Only seven of the ten C28 speedboats engaged August the 18th's second unit. Three of their boats had broken away from the main pack and were still propelling at a steady pace towards the incoming cargo ships. Eliza noticed from her position on top of the cockpit. In particular she spotted three large soldierly individuals on one of the boats. They sat side by side shrouded by black raincoats with long spears leaning over their right shoulders. Even from their hoods, Eliza could make out the long black dreadlocks that came down past their necks and over their chests. She then looked out to the west. The cargo ships were closing in from 800 meters out and slowing down. Priest Edwin and the rest of unit one already had the boats in the water and were waiting for her.

"Robby. Which boat is it? Can you pick anything up on infrared?" Eliza stressed with concern.

Robby sat in his chair helpless and frustrated as he stared intensely at his computer screen. Even with the skills at his disposal, it seems he couldn't give Eliza what she needed. The screen showed the three freight ships, but each ship showed the same blue green cold of a soulless vacancy. Biting on his lips, he simply shook his head no. He didn't have the heart to admit what he perceived to be a failure. Austin and Stephen noticed and with Austin patting him on the back.

"Jag. The containers are probably all insulated with a layer of nitrous-fiber glass. These containers aren't vulnerable to our satellites picking up their heat signatures. Some shippers use these kinds of containers to keep electronics safe from powerful x-ray scans. It isn't unusual." Stephen informed them through the radio.

"This means we're on our own, Jaguar. Forget about the blasted computers and satellites. The best defense is a strong offense. You said you'd trust in us. So trust us." Priest Edwin pleaded.

The three separate C28 boats had just picked up speed toward the cargo ships. Eliza looked down into Priest's cold blue eyes. With a quick nod to herself, she dropped down fifteen feet from the cockpit onto the pavement. Her men started the motors as Eliza ran and hopped into a boat next to the one Priest was in. On her order, the three boats took off heading west.

The three cargo ships now had their propellers in reverse to bring their speed to a halt. Eliza and her first unit were closing in on the vessels almost at an L-shaped ninety-degree angle that was perpendicular to the enemy. The C28 boats were heading directly for the cargo ship's front bow while August the 18th was approaching the left side of the closest of the three ships.

"This isn't good! We need to know which one!" An 18th Soldier behind Priest Edwin shouted as the inflatable boats hopped up and down over the surface of the wavy dark waters.

Eliza closed her eyes. As the cold icy sprays of salt water splashed up and scraped against her facemask and forehead, she concentrated on her hearing. Through the relentless pops of gunfire and men shouting out toward the east, through the kicking whips of the boat engines running at full throttle, Eliza focused on the cargo ships and listened to the hollow hum of the ship directly in front of her. After listening to it for close to five seconds, she came to a reasonable conclusion that there was no life aboard that ship and that it must be controlled remotely.

"This isn't it!" She shouted just as she noticed the C28 boats had maneuvered dangerously in-between the middle of the three ships.

"Priest, take the boats and head around the back. We can narrow it down to either the middle ship or the one on the far south side. Go!" She ordered.

Priest Edwin nodded as he watched Eliza leaned over and pick up a large repelling grabbling gun. "Wait, Jag! What are you going to do?" He shouted.

While centering herself low in the inflatable boat, Eliza used both arms to hoist up and aim a grappling gun high towards the bow of the ship that was now protruding above them. "I trust you, Priest. You guys will be alright." She shouted back.

With that, Eliza fired. A puff of dirty smoke expelled as the high-powered grappling gun shot out a hook that harpooned through a metal panel in the bow just below the deck railing. With the click of a thumb button, pieces of the grappling gun detached off until all that was left was just a gripping handle bar and a reel. Eliza held onto the handle bar using only her right hand as the reel began to retract the grappling cable. The force of the reel launched Eliza high into the air, swinging her toward the front of the ship.

Whilst soaring through the air, Eliza used the thumb button to slow down the recoiling speed of the retracting cables. Kicking both of her legs forward, Eliza was able to swing around the front of the ship in between the three massive cargo ships. The men in one of the C28 speedboats noticed her behind them. They immediately opened fire. Bullets whisked past her and some cut through her overcoat. Just as Eliza was about to bounce off the starboard side, she pulled on the cable to lift her legs up to touch her heels onto the ship's starboard side. Keeping with the same momentum of the swing, Eliza held on to the grapple handle with her right hand and sprinted along the side of the ship toward the Haitian gunmen.

With her left hand, Eliza reached into her coat pocket and pulled out two of Robby's makeshift ninja star grenades. She activated the grenades by pushing a button in the center of the stars. Gradually the six Haitians in the boat stopped shooting and simply stood with astonishment as Eliza's speed surpassed their own. She ran past their small vessel on the water beneath her as a mixture of pure adrenaline kicked in along with her Furyx. In a dangerous move Eliza let go of the grappling cord. Sliding along the wet metal ship panels with her body almost virtually horizontal, she squatted to plant both boots in a single spot and launched herself away from the cargo ship.

Eliza spiraled as she soared through the air. The Haitians stood stupefied at the sight of her flying directly above them; none of them noticing that she had flipped two spiked grenades onto the boat deck near their feet. After flying out of three fast acrobatic flips, Eliza landed with a rolling summersault over the surface of a wet container from the middle cargo ship. Five seconds later, a booming explosion rang out with a watery spray of blood, limbs, and guns spraying out across the freezing surface of the gulf.

Slightly distracted by the satisfaction of her own handy work, Eliza snapped back only after a bullet clipped the top of her left shoulder. With the throbbing pain instantly shooting through, she quickly whipped around to face her attackers. Her eyes widened with anticipation at the sight. The near eighteen Haitian men from the remaining two speedboats had embarked onto the same ship she was on. They had already spread throughout the ship and were frantically searching the twenty-foot metal shipping containers one by one. The Inca Trinity were standing side by side on the bridge of the ship, waiting like statues with their spears leaning against their pectorals. Four August the 18th soldiers finally managed to climb onto the railing of the ship near their position and began opening fire.

"No! Stand down!" Eliza shouted as she raced towards them in a dash.

She would be too late. As soon as they were fired upon, the three spear fighters of the Inca Trinity sprang into motion, whipping off their black raincoats. The three large, muscular men were bare foot, bare-chested and identical triplets. They were wearing only baggy dark camouflaged pants as they whirled their spears and closed in on the four 18th soldiers. Almost with ease, the spear fighters used their evasive capoeira dance to move in and cut down the four 18th soldiers despite being shot at close range by live rounds.

"Pull back!" Eliza shouted at the rest of her unit.

The rest of the first unit had just boarded the vessel and some were unfortunate enough to catch the last moments of their comrades falling to their deaths. Enraged, Priest Edwin held up his M16 assault rifle, aimed down the sights and fired at one of the Inca Trinity. The 5.5 mm bullet hit its target directly in the back of the neck. Any normal man would've collapsed half decapitated on the spot. But the spear fighter simply dropped down to one knee, holding his head as if he were just hit with a baseball bat. Much to Priest Edwin's horror, the spear fighter wasn't even bleeding. Unbeknownst to the priest, the bullet had managed to stun him, cutting the reaction time in his nervous system by half and slowing the use of his legs.

Inca Trinity snarled as they regrouped around their fallen, lifted him up, and slowly closed in on Priest Edwin and the line of men flanking him.

"Protect the women and children. Find the indivisualist. I'll handle this." Priest said as he dropped his gun and pulled out his extendable golden staff.

You too!" Eliza shouted.

Five ninja stars whistled through the air to stick into the deck's metal flooring between the 18th and the spear fighters. Almost in unison, all of the men turned to see Eliza leap off of a shipping container, reach for the bridge's railing and flip herself up directly in the path of the Inca Trinity.

"Remember what I said. No civic casualties." Eliza told them.

"Fan out and eliminate them. Weapons tight. Let's go!" Priest instructed to his men.

After a nod to his female commander, Priest jumped over a railing onto the deck with the rest of the first unit right behind him. The deck of the ship felt like a maze with the men weaving between the large twenty-foot metal shipping containers. There were eighty containers on this particular ship and the Haitians had already managed to open thirty-two. One by one, August the 18th began picking off the C28 gang wherever they encountered them.

The three tall, dark and grim spear fighters watched dumbfounded as Eliza took off her hooded raincoat and tossed it to the side. Her sleek skintight wetsuit glistened in the illumination from the stadium lights that flooded over the bay. The green in her eyes squinted with a smile as she popped her neck to the side to loosen up.

"Capoeira.... I know a little something about that. You guys don't speak any English do you? Figures..." She said.

One of the spear fighters smiled at her with a bobbing nod. "Run home and get some sleep little girl. We don't kill the beautiful ladies." The spear fighter said in a casual Jamaican accent. His teeth had black voodoo symbols carved in them.

Eliza rolled her eyes and shook her head, irked at the fact that he thought his words were cool. Slowly, she brought her right foot back into a run stance squat and reached for the handle of her Ivy ninja sword that was hanging down by her lower back. The Inca Trinity noticed and gripped their spears for the ready.

Taking the initiative to engage the Inca, Eliza gave a lightning face wave of her right hand to whip out the last ninja star she had in her possession. Due to random sparks of gunfire popping off around them, one of the spear fighters failed to see the razor sharp edge until it was too late. The ninja star was the size of a business card and it was now lodged halfway through the socket of his left eye. The spear fighter instantly dropped his spear and let out loud agonizing scream as he reached for his left eye.

The remaining two spear fighters reached for him with genuine concern and empathy. Staying low in an impulse dash, Eliza closed the distance on them in the blink of an eye. Despite this, the two able-bodied spear fighters were able to pull their carbon fiber metal spears up in time to block her first few strikes.

She then performed a one-handed cartwheel to move in between them. It was a good strategy. The spear fighters had to limit their attacks to short quick thrusts and exercise caution to avoid striking each other. It was a terrific battle. From a balcony view, it appeared to be a battle between two black spiders attacking a smaller green spider. Rubber scruffs marked the wet steel deck as grunts and blade whistles surrounded them.

The spear fighters had years of experience under their belt and possessed more strength and dexterity. They kept aiming for her head, but Eliza was ten times more agile and quicker with her swings. Showing off a seemingly endless a variety of cartwheels and aerial contortions, Eliza was able to dodge their spears and dish out her own relentless counters that kept the Inca from relaxing even for a second. The Furyx users were so fast, their swings so powerful. When their blades were in motion all anyone could make out were brief flashes of light. And their blades were in constant motion.

The three minutes were up. Two thirty-foot red vessels representing the Coast Guard were already breaking across the waves towards Slater and Sinus's gunfight. Brian and the 3rd Unit were all laying prone on the rooftop of a warehouse overlooking the bay. The telescopic lenses on their rifles were programmed to automatically zoom in on any heat signatures. So one by one, Brian and the 18th Soldiers began sniping at the Coast Guard with beanbags, dropping their targets with mild concussions and leaving their vessels to drift idle.

The nautical battle between Slater's 2nd Unit and the C28 militia was thinning out. Five of the seven Haitian boats were in the process of sinking with their occupants struggling to stay above the surface of the water. The second unit had suffered three casualties with twelve more men injured from bullet flesh wounds. Slater ordered two boats to hang back and retrieved two soldiers that fell overboard. And Sinus was proceeding to chase down the last two Haitian vessels. Slater made it clear that they were not giving them the option to retreat. The loss of his men brought back vindictive memories and he was not about to let them hit and run.

On the cargo ship, Priest led the 1st Unit weaving between the rows of containers in proper military fashion. Seeing that their comrades were being picked off one by one, the opposing C28 had no choice but to stop their search of the containers and contend with the men of the 18th.

In the midst of the gunfight, the latch of a door to a particular container was popped open. This container was double-stacked on top of another one with no other container in front of it. There were forty-six Mexican women and children packed into this container. The timid Madison Mariana Rios cautiously peeked out to see what was going on.

Because this container was one of six stacked on top of another, he couldn't see the first unit duking it out with C28 on the deck below. All he could hear were the constant gunshots. But he did see a blonde woman in the distance holding her own against two larger black muscular men with dreadlocks. Madison was baffled. While he was terrified of the unknown, he couldn't take his eyes off of Eliza.

In the midst of her sword fight, Eliza had just managed to parry a lunge aimed for her face. Just as she was swiping a spear away, another fighter moved in and planted his heel into her chest with a perfectly executed butterfly kick. The force of the kick sent Eliza flying backwards into the railing causing her to flip over and hit the main deck twelve feet below the bridge. She felt a rush of pain shoot up from her right ankle and released a strained grunt as she looked to see if it was twisted. Just as she looked back up, a spear fighter was falling towards her. She impulsively dashed to her left, but the spear fighter still managed to bring the tip of his spear down to cut her right shoulder.

Eliza rolled on the wet freezing metal as the other two spear fighters jumped over the railing to continue. She was sweating hard. The stinging pain in her right shoulder was intense, causing her right arm to rattle and her grip to weaken. Despite this, she quickly sheathed her sword and did a series of back handsprings to create distance between them. The spear fighters gave chase. As Eliza came close to the containers behind her, she pushed off of the floor in the midst of a handspring to perform an impressive fifteen-foot high vaulting backflip to land on the top of the first row of containers.

The spear fighters were getting frustrated. It's never taken them that long to kill anyone, not to mention it was three against one. With a synchronized roar of anger the spear fighters ran forward and leaped up to pull themselves onto the wet containers like rampaging gorillas. With a squinty-eyed glare, Eliza breathed the fumes out of her nostrils, waiting in a squat ready to pounce.

The spear fighter with the ninja star still lodged in his blood-gushing left eye ran for Eliza first. But halfway to Eliza, the spear fighter misjudged his depth perception in midstride and stumbled on the wet surface of the container top. Like a shark sensing blood, Eliza rushed to capitalize, leaping up from her squatting position to plunge the tip of her sword into the man's throat.

One of the brothers saw this and was overcome with blind rage and grief. Eliza stood casual with her hand on the sword handle that was still penetrating a quarter into the man's throat. With her strength, she continued to hold him up, prolonging the pain. Her eyes were wide open as she stared at the remaining two spear fighters, like a territorial jaguar that sensed intruders. They could hear their identical brother gurgling for help with blood rushing out of the wound in his neck.

With a loud war cry, the closest spear fighter rushed forward. Eliza ripped out her sword, sending a spray of scarlet from the man's throat into her attacker's eyes. Again, seizing the opportunity from the spear fighter's temporary blindness, Eliza evaded his wild desperate swings and moved in. His death came when she dragged the sharp edge of Ivy in a horizontal swing to rip open his abdomen. Two spear fighters dropped dead at the same time with Eliza waiting in a low ninja stance glaring at the last spear fighter. Her blade hungered for more.

Fear finally set in with the dark mercenary. He knew he was staring directly at an animal that would counter whatever he did and sink in her fangs. Then suddenly, something caught the Inca's eye. To his right he saw Madison Mariana Rio poking his head outside the container. It was his target staring him right in the face. His brothers died in their mission to kill that one man. He couldn't allow their deaths to go in vain. With an insane burst of rage, the spear fighter gripped his spear and burst into a wild sprint as fast has he could.

Just one container away from his target, the Inca launched himself into an impressive twenty-foot leap with a menacing snarl. He pulled his spear back in preparation for one final throw but he'd never get a chance to release it. As his body was flying outstretched in midair, a sudden jolt of force abruptly caused his body to slam face first into a scraping halt on container surface just five feet in front of Madison. Eliza was sitting mounted on the Haitian's back. Both hands were tightly wrapped around the handle of her sword. The blade of Ivy was driven deep into the man's spine just below the back of his neck.

As the spear fighter leaped for Madison, Eliza had leaped for the spear fighter. In mid-air, she executed a front flip and managed to swing her legs as hard as she could when she came out of that flip. This added the momentum she needed to catch up and get in close to wrap her legs around the spear fighter's waist and plunge in her sword before slamming the mercenary onto the container with a hollow echoing metallic boom.

After taking a brief moment to catch her breath, Eliza slowly rose to stand up. She could hear the grinding of bone in his vertebrae as she pulled out her blood soaked sword. Her head was burning hot with a headache. Her wetsuit donned dozens of acute cuts along her obliques and thigh but only the bleeding wound to her shoulder required medical condition. Even from her training in the mountains with the ninjas, she had never experienced a fight like this before. She had underestimated her opponents. A lesson she'd do well to remember.

Then she looked straight ahead and noticed Madison was staring at her. He stood frozen in place, petrified by the kill that was reminiscent to nature films of big cats dragging down their prey.

"Jag!" An 18th Member shouted.

Eliza whipped to her left to see a single C28 member aiming an assault rifle at her. The three August the 18th soldiers who saw him were out of bullets and running as fast as they could to reach him. Glistening with cold sweat, the Haitian let out a spray of bullets before he was brought down by an arrow from Priest Edwin's crossbow. Eliza was struck several times. One bullet hit her across the face, knocking off the facemask. Two other bullets popped her across her left ribcage just below the breast. The force of which, knocked her off balance and caused her to drop her to one knee.

"Jaguar!" Nell, an 18th soldier with a long dark beard that came past his own facemask shouted as he ran to Eliza's side.

"I'm fine. I'm fine." Eliza said.

She stood up and leaned right to stretch out her left oblique pop a rib back into place. Priest Edwin walked over and put both hands on her shoulders to face him. Without saying a word he took hold of the zipper beneath her chin and aggressively unzipped the battle-torn wetsuit.

"Edwin? What are you?" Eliza asked, feeling slightly violated as her white sports bra was now exposed.

"Hey what's going on? It's quiet out there. What's happened? Is everyone alright?" Brian called over the radio.

"No! Dan, Matt and Kirkpatrick are dead." Slater responded in anguish. "But we're clear on our end. All tangos down."

"What about the hostages?" Robby asked.

Priest pulled Eliza's wet suit down to her waist to examine her tan skin. He was stunned to see there was only a dark reddish bruise where the bullets hit her. But he was confused as to how the blade from a spear managed to cut her right shoulder. Priest dropped his cross bow and took out a field knife to cut off a strip of his shirt. The other 18th soldiers from 1st Unit walked towards Madison and the container.

The long bearded 18th soldier, Nell, approached Madison's container and pulled it open. "It's alright. You're safe now." He said.

Nell then turned to look at other 18th soldiers. Taking charge, Nell told the others to fan out and open the other containers. The other immigrants couldn't have been too far from Madison's. The 1st Unit would go on to open up five double stacked TEU containers, all containing women and children. The occupants were all swirling with a combination of gratitude, terror and confusion. No one was hurt. But everyone was cold and starving.

"Slater. Sinus. Please, bring your units over to our position. We need to dock this ship and get these hostages off as soon as possible." Eliza ordered calmly.

The relief of success was just now starting to set in. In the heat of battle, Eliza couldn't think of anything other than the overwhelming opponents in front of her. To be able to lower her shoulders from that intensity took almost as much effort as it did to prepare for it. Luckily there was an 18th member in the 1st Unit who had some experienced with handling boats. He took over the controls and safely guided the ship towards the berths. Meanwhile, Priest was still examining Eliza. He used a strip of his shirtsleeve to tie up the cut on her shoulder.

"Let's get going, Priest." Eliza told him, slightly unnerved that she was just tended to.

"I do not understand. The Furyx users have more power than a speeding bullet?" Priest asked.

"I don't know. Right now, we need to get these people to dry land." Eliza said pulling up her wetsuit and zipping up.

"Hey Jag!" An 18th member called out.

The member was holding her dark-green rain coat. He threw it up to her from the main deck. Eliza caught it with both hands but it was soaked with sea water. Squeezing it out, the strength of her grasp caused a sharp spritz of water to hit her in the face. Several members looking on couldn't help but laugh at her, including some of the Mexican children who hadn't smiled in days.

Eliza had an extra face mask in one of the coat pockets. She pulled it out and put it on before turning to Madison. The activist was still gawking at her as if he had seen a ghost. For the entire two day voyage he was dressed in humble clothing, most likely to blend in and seem less significant than the women and children he accompanied.

Eliza nodded, understanding his astonishment. "You've seen my face. But I feel like I can trust you, Mr. Madison Rios. We are August the 18th. At your service."

Madison approached with caution and gave a deep heartfelt bow toward Eliza and Priest. "Words…I uh…Words cannot express our gratitude. We owe you our lives." Madison said in his Hispanic-tinted accent.

"Your life belongs to you, Senor Rios. We're just happy to help preserve it." Priest Edwin replied.

Eliza nodded before looking past him. The women and children in the container behind him were still sitting, huddled and gripped with traumatic apprehension. One of them stood out to Eliza. There was a teenager of middle school age. She was Mexican but her hair was dyed blond with a pair of complimenting natural stone-green eyes. Her cheeks were puffy with pits under her eyes swollen from recent tears. With goose bumps peppering her arms, her back was against the container wall. And in those arms she held onto her younger sister who couldn't have been much older than six.

The 18th men carried food and water in their duffle bags and were already in the process of distribution. Eliza removed her sword strap from around her waist and handed it to Priest. An 18th soldier instinctively read her emotions and handed her a water bottle and bag of shortbread cookies. She thanked the soldier and walked to the pair of sisters.

Priest Edwin approached Madison. "Have you heard of us?"

Madison's head turned from Eliza to the eerie voice of Priest. "Um…Yes. Well, I had heard of a group calling themselves August the 18th. I heard you were all ninjas only interested in fighting gangs and stealing from the mob. Which is why I'm slightly confused as to why you'd risk your life to save the likes of us."

Eliza kneeled in front of the blond teenager and her sister. She cautiously extended the water bottle to the teenager. Still weary, but more so thirsty, the teen reluctantly accepted. Eliza couldn't help but smile, satisfied and pleased to do a good deed. She handed the little sister a cookie. The less cynical sister gratefully accepted the cookie with a giggling smile. Eliza noticed an elderly woman next to the sisters with her arm wrapped in a sling. She handed her a cookie as well.

"That girl there is our commander, the fabled green-eyed jaguar. The rumors are true. She is a ninja. And while it appears that we're just dismantling gangs and picking a fight with corrupt officials, our ambitions run much deeper than that." Priest told Madison.

"Why do you call yourselves August the 18th? I knew Reginald Harvey. He was my friend. If he knew such a group had taken the name of his most prized works and used it in this way, he would most likely roll over in his grave." Madison said sternly before letting out a sharp congested cough.

Priest slowly turned his head to look at Eliza. She was still handing out cookies and water as if she were tending to sheltered puppies. He understood Madison's question and nodded before answering.

"The book saved her life. As an indivisualist no one can fully understand the motives of another. We can guess. We can speculate. But there's no way one can truly know. No matter what someone says they can do or their reasons for doing it, it all boils down to their actions. Sometimes common sense is the only real truth one needs to know. What lies beneath the surface, is *beneath* the surface for a reason. Malcolm X and Martin Luther King Jr. had similar goals, but went about it in different ways. You can speak and preach about change and progress till you're blue in the face. August the 18th is the force that enacts change. I'm sure an intellect like you can figure out the rest."

Madison Rios still wore a puzzled expression. He had about a dozen logical arguments in his arsenal to debunk the priest's words…but it was hard to impress those arguments given the circumstance. Thus, he practiced the exercise of letting others to continue believing that they are right.

"I am a man who once captivated a stadium audience filled to capacity. And yet, I was still forced to leave my home. Forced to leave the people who once cheered my name and claimed to believe in me. Where were they when I was arrested and the government labeled me a traitor? Sure, my followers were afraid to speak out for me. But then again…so is August the 18th. They have to be. Compared to home, Tampa Bay is a penitentiary full of gangs where everyone has some allegiance to the underworld. Yet, they stand up and fight. Risk their lives. All following a young woman."

These were the thoughts swirling in Madison's head as he watched August the 18th help the women and children of his homeland.

The cargo ship was safely docked at a berth at 2:11am. Much to Eliza's dismay, Brian and Priest persuaded her that the group needed to disperse before the tranquilizers wear off and security guards become un-concussed. While their mission was a success in warding an attack from the syndicate, it was a disastrous mess that left yet another stinging slap in the face of law enforcement, one that reporters and media outlets couldn't help but dine on.

The Port Authority ended up pulling twenty-eight dead C28 gang members from the bay and arresting twelve more who were injured and left behind by their fleeing comrades. Madison Mariana Rios and all 138 Mexican women and children were rescued and put under the protection of the Imperial government as dictated by the Mexican-America pact agreement of 2182.

While the immigrants were sent to an undisclosed residential neighborhood somewhere south of Tallahassee, Madison was able to continue his activism, guarded by the Imperial Secret Service. Over the next few months, Eliza and August the 18th would continue to keep watch over the immigrant's new community as their self-anointed guardians. In the back of her mind, Eliza would never forget that blond Mexican teenager. Hoping to one day recruit her as a protégé.

It was the first mission where August the 18th suffered casualties. It was already discussed how they would handle the dead. Secrecy of the group would remain each member's priority even in death. As such, each member was well aware that their deaths would be staged to look like accidents to shroud their activities with a vigilante militia. For the members who were shot, their bodies would turn up days later in a rough neighborhood to look like a robbery. For those who drowned, they're bodies would wash up days later to appear as if they planned their own suicide. The family members of the departed were never to know of the true circumstances surrounding their deaths. They would never know that they were once part of the intrepid August the 18th.

About Stage in the Sky

Revenge, Rivalry and Rebellion, Stage in the Sky is the theater that presents the entertaining stories and essays of neo-romanticist Rock Kitaro.

When I was fifteen, I read three books that would forever change my life. The most significant was Nancy Springer's "I am Mordred." If you know your Arthurian Legend then you know that Mordred is the name of the knight who kills King Arthur. But Nancy Springer's book told the story from Mordred's point of view. It told of his upbringing, his love, his ambitions.

It was amazing. Reading her book opened my eyes to the world of perspective. Before this, and even now, it seems so many people these days forget that there are two sides or more sides to every story. Even the worst villains are heroes to somebody else. No one just rolls out of bed with a desire to cause harm. And even if they do, there's a reason. So why not let the audience decide if that reason is good enough. This is what I do with my stories.

I'll go ahead and tell you that with my stories, I curse and can sometimes be choreographic with my fight scenes. Inspired by Lord Byron, all of my main characters are troubled individuals. They are sophisticated, arrogant, seductive, disrespectful of authority, self-destructive and struggle with a sense of integrity, what's right or wrong.

Make sure to visit **www.stageinthesky.com** for Rock Kitaro's latest releases or send your regards to RockKitaro@gmail.com.

The Three Kings of Ybor Saga

Vol. 1 – Eliza Christie's Vendetta

Vol. 2 – The Wolves of the Syndicate

Vol. 3 – A Reunion of Beasts

Vol. 4 – August the 18th

Vol. 5 – The Kennedy St. Massacre

Vol. 6 – Beware of Romanticists

Vol. 7 – The Ides of March

www.ingramcontent.com/pod-product-compliance
Lightning Source LLC
Chambersburg PA
CBHW060627130626
46555CB00002B/693